Their bodies were pressed so closely together it was as if they were one person instead of two. Then Luke pulled some fancy footwork on her, spinning Joanne around so that her back was against his chest as he pushed himself against her buttocks. Unable to resist, Joanne continued to move with him, savoring the sensation of his rock hard frame kissing the cushion of her soft curves. She raised her arms over her head, dancing against him, her fingers snapping in time to the music.

Luke slipped his arms back around her waist, spinning her around to face him. The look in his eyes was pure, unadulterated lust, and his hunger set every nerve ending in Joanne's body on fire. As Luke continued to move against her, his left arm holding her tightly around the waist, his right hand moved up the length of her back and his palm came to rest against the back of her head. Without warning, Luke slipped his fingers into the short length of her hair as he dipped her over his arm.

The gesture took Joanne by surprise, causing her to gasp loudly, right before Luke leaned down over her, pressing his mouth against the curve of her neck. The sensation of his lips against her bare skin was overwhelming and Joanne moaned out loud, almost forgetting that they were surrounded by a crowd of people. As he lifted her back up, Luke smiled and wrapped both of his arms around her as he pressed his cheek to hers.

He whispered into her ear, his breath blowing hot against her flesh. "I'd say that was just my intro to foreplay. To give you a full definition, though, I would need a whole weekend alone with you."

Books by Deborah Fletcher Mello

Kimani Romance

In the Light of Love
Always Means Forever
To Love a Stallion
Tame a Wild Stallion
Lost in a Stallion's Arms

Kimani Arabesque

Take Me to Heart
A Love for All Time
The Right Side of Love
Forever and a Day
Love in the Lineup

DEBORAH FLETCHER MELLO

has been writing since she was thirteen years old and can't imagine herself doing anything else. Her first romance novel, *Take Me to Heart*, earned her a 2004 Romance Slam Jam nomination for Best New Author. In 2005 she received Book of the Year and Favorite Heroine nominations for her novel *The Right Side of Love*, and in 2009 she won an *RT Book Reviews* Reviewers' Choice Award for her ninth novel, *Tame a Wild Stallion*.

For Deborah, writing is akin to breathing and she firmly believes that if she could not write she would cease to exist. Weaving a story that leaves her audience feeling full and complete, as if they've just enjoyed an incredible meal, is the ultimate thrill for her. Born and raised in Connecticut, Deborah now maintains base camp in North Carolina but considers home to be wherever the moment moves her.

Lost IN A STALLION'S Arms

DEBORAH FLETCHER MELLO

KIMANI™
ROMANCE

To my very special friend,
Thank you for the inspiration.
I love you.
Now and always.

 KIMANI PRESS™

Recycling programs
for this product may
not exist in your area.

ISBN-13: 978-0-373-86163-7

LOST IN A STALLION'S ARMS

www.kimanipress.com

Printed in U.S.A.

Dear Reader,

The Stallion men are back and it doesn't get any better than this!

After a two-year hiatus I am so excited to bring you the next installment in my romantic series starring those billionaire brothers, Matthew, Mark, Luke and John Stallion.

I loved writing every bit of Luke's story. The boy is twentysomething, young and every bit a stallion stud. He is a walking sex machine, bringing much pleasure to the vivacious Joanne Lake, a full-figured beauty who captures his heart.

I have been living and breathing the Stallion men for months now, and with each one I find myself more in love with the idea of love. I so hope that you enjoy getting to know each Stallion brother and that you fall in love with my Texas boys just like I have.

Thank you for continuing to support me on this amazing journey. Your thoughts of encouragement keep me writing and motivate me to write well. There aren't enough words to express how much I value each of you.

You can keep up with me at www.deborahmello.blogspot.com.

Until the next time, take care and God bless.

With much love,

Deborah Fletcher Mello

Chapter 1

At six o'clock, when his morning alarm clock sounded, Luke Stallion was already standing beneath the heated spray of his morning shower. Six perfectly positioned stainless-steel showerheads were pelting water over every square inch of his muscular body.

Maneuvering the shower massage feature, Luke adjusted the spray until the pressurized water felt like hundreds of sturdy fingers were kneading the tension out of his very taut body. Closing his eyes, Luke tilted his head forward, allowing the water to rain down over his closely cropped haircut and beat against the back of his thick neck. As he tilted his head back again, the water hit him in the face with full force and pounded against his broad chest.

A rise of steam billowed in the open space, painting the tiled walls with a cloudy mist. Minutes passed before Luke moved to soap himself with the organic body wash he favored. He took a deep breath, inhaling the scent of sandalwood and vanilla, and just like that he was wide-eyed and awake, his earlier moments of sluggishness vanquished.

Luke was suddenly anxious about the mandatory meeting that had been scheduled for first thing that day. The memo had said no one was excused, and he could only begin to imagine what was so important. Having spent most of the night brushing up on the details of all his current projects, Luke was fairly confident that he would be able to respond to anything thrown at him, but then again, with his older brothers, just how sure could he be? He heaved a deep sigh.

Reaching for his requisite loofah sponge, he guided his large hands across the tight, sinewy lines of his torso. The soft sponge gently caressed his flesh, his skin like dark satin stretched over rock-hard marble. As he soaped and lathered each taut muscle, Luke had the overwhelming sensation that something big was going to happen to him today. Something that would change his life forever. He only wished he had a clue what that was so that he could be prepared for it.

Luke heaved a deep sigh. Leaning forward, he pressed his palms against the tile, the spray washing over his back and buttocks. Beaded water like tiny pearls tolled down his back, puddling in small streams before running down the backs of his long legs.

Some thirty minutes later he stepped from the shower, reaching for a large white towel that rested on the corner of the marble countertop. As he swiped at the moisture that dampened his skin, he admired his reflection in the mirror. His time in the gym was paying off nicely, definition clearly painting the muscular lines of his body. The new trainer was working him well, and Luke appreciated the benefits the hard work was producing.

Wrapping the towel around his waist, he stood staring at his reflection for a minute longer. Energy gleamed in the pools of black gold that were his eyes. They were his father's eyes, and his brothers'. History glimmered back at him, a testament to the legacy he'd been bequeathed at birth. He was a true Stallion, through and through. Never mind him being prepared for whatever was coming. Whatever was coming had better be prepared for him, Luke mused, a soft smile pulling at his mouth. Nothing and no one had ever bested a Stallion man, and as far as he was concerned, nothing and no one ever would.

The laughter ringing through the conference room of Stallion Enterprises' corporate headquarters belied the serious nature of the business meeting the executive board was supposed to be holding. The Stallion brothers, Matthew, Mark, Luke and John, were chuckling heartily as they sat discussing the impending anniversary celebrations for Mark, John and John's father-in-law, Edward Briscoe. It had been one year since all three men had jumped the holy matrimony broom, each of them taking a wife within weeks of each other.

The joint anniversary celebration had been the brain child of John's wife, Marah, and her twin sister, Eden Waller. Mark's wife, Michelle, had been pulled into the excitement, albeit reluctantly—the other women were adamant that since Edward and his wife, Juanita, and Michelle and Mark had both eloped, then their one-year anniversary celebrations needed to be the talk of Dallas. The three-day event was scheduled to coincide with the family reunion and the annual Black Rodeo hosted by the Briscoe-Stallion family at the renowned Briscoe Ranch.

"I swear," John was exclaiming, disconnecting the call on his personal cell phone. "This party is going to send us to the poor house. Every time Marah calls it's about the price of something having gone up. This thing is costing a fortune!" The man tossed up his arms, feigning annoyance.

His brothers all laughed, three pairs of dark eyes focused on his wide grin. The family resemblance ran deep, all four men imposing in stature. They each boasted well-formed physiques, black-coffee complexions, chiseled jawlines, seductive bedroom eyes and charismatic smiles.

Luke laughed. "I can't believe you and Mark keep giving in so easily. Those women have both of you whipped silly!"

Mark laughed with him. "Love will do that to you, baby brother. You should try it."

Luke shook his head from side to side. "Not me. I'm following in Matthew's footsteps." He gestured in his brother's direction. "You go, Mr. Bachelor of the Year!" he exclaimed, acknowledging their sibling's most recent claim to fame.

Matthew laughed. "That's right, baby brother! Don't go out like that. Enjoy it while you can!"

"What do you mean?" Mark asked. "Go out like what? John and I didn't do anything but get married."

"And married to very beautiful, talented, exceptional women," John added. "I have to tell you boys, it beats that dating game you two want to keep playing."

Luke's head waved from side to side. "I like that game. I play it very well."

"Me, too, as evidenced by the fact *Texan* magazine is giving me an award for it," Matthew intoned. "In fact," he said, gazing down at the Rolex watch on his wrist, "I plan to play with Miss Daphne Cuthbert at seven o'clock this evening, so let's get this meeting wrapped up."

"Does Daphne have any sisters?" Luke queried.

Matthew nodded enthusiastically, gesturing with his hands. "As a matter of fact, her sister, Janette, has a pair of legs that go from here to—"

John held up his hand. "Spare us." He chuckled. "You two are determined to learn your lessons the hard way," he said, his head shaking from side to side. "Don't say Mark and I didn't warn you!" Shifting the stack of manila folders on the table in front of him, John laughed heartily, his brothers laughing with him. "On to new business," he said, shifting back into CEO mode without batting an eye.

Not skipping a beat, his siblings shifted with him, their earlier elation replaced with disciplined reservation. John leaned back in his leather executive's chair, his arms folding over his chest as his gaze shifted from one brother to another. His forehead was furrowed as he fell into deep thought, something serious clearly crossing his mind. The other three men leaned forward, each of them attentive. Luke pulled his yellow-lined notepad closer, his ballpoint pen poised in anticipation.

John began slowly. "The reason I called this meeting is because Stallion stock has been under accumulation over the last few weeks. Too swiftly and too much of it. It's raising some concerns about who is suddenly so interested in us and why."

"Isn't interest a good thing?" Luke asked, meeting John's gaze evenly. "It's near an all-time high, isn't it?

John nodded. "That's true, but it's not a good thing if it's all being purchased for the wrong reasons. One entity in control of too many shares could present us with some major problems."

Matthew nodded. "Word on the street is someone wants us and wants us bad. We have to figure out who and why. I'll be contacting all of our major stockholders in the next few weeks to see if anyone can shed any light on the situation, but we can't afford to let our guard down. This could be a problem for us."

A look of confusion crossed Luke's face. "I don't understand…" he started.

"We four have controlling interest in the company right now, but if one individual acquires enough of our stock, we could find ourselves in the middle of a hostile takeover attempt," John answered.

Mark shook his head. "No one would be that bold, would they?

John shrugged. "Anything is possible, but no matter what, we need to make sure we're on top of our game in case this gets ugly. We've all worked too hard to get where we are. We will not lose this company."

There was a pregnant pause as each man fell into his own thoughts, remembrances of Stallion Enterprises' growth and their individual contributions to the company crossing their minds.

John hadn't yet graduated from Morehouse College in Atlanta before he'd begun negotiations for his very first acquisition. He'd formulated a solid business plan, the base of it grounded in determination and an adventurous spirit. Taking a chance on a small complex of rental units in foreclosure, he'd financed the deal with his share of the insurance money they'd all received after the untimely death of their parents. After investing a small sum of money to renovate and upgrade the property, he'd sold it some four months later for a sizeable profit. The rest had been history.

Building a financially secure future for his younger siblings had been foremost in John's mind, his determination motivating him to move mountains for his family's survival. Stallion Enterprises was now a respected corporate empire built on commercial real estate and development as well as a shipping company, with entertainment interests, and Mark's newest pet project, a nationally ranked professional race team. Success had come after much hard work.

As the company had grown, John had ensured that his parents' dreams of each of them attending and graduating from college had come true. Matthew had attended Harvard on a full academic scholarship, later earning a juris doctorate from Harvard's prestigious school of law. Mark had followed John to Morehouse, graduating with honors and a dual degree in engineering and physics.

And then there'd been Luke. The baby of the family had finally graduated from Texas Southern University with a degree in business management. Luke had done the six-year program, his two freshman years causing John much angst as the young man's focus had been on everything but his studies. And each of them had eventually thrown their hats into the Stallion ring, committing themselves fully to the company.

Looking around the table, John couldn't help but smile. His dreams come true had been more than even he had imagined. John knew their parents would have been proud. His gaze fell on Luke, who returned his smile as if he'd been able to read the older man's thoughts.

John turned his attention back to business. "Let's move on," he said softly.

A stack of manila folders rested in the center of the table. John pulled one file in particular from the heap waiting for his attention. He studied the typed file label only briefly before handing the profile of documentation to Luke. Leaning back in the cushioned executive's chair, John clasped his hands together in his lap. He nodded his head in Luke's direction, and the young man's eyes widened with a mix of curiosity and rising excitement as his older brother began to speak.

"Luke, you've been doing an excellent job for us. Your work has been truly impressive. We were thrilled with the results you managed to attain with the union negotiations. Both sides have commended your actions. As well, the legal department had some good things to say about what you did on that last acquisition."

Luke's lips bent into a slight smile as his other siblings nodded their agreement.

John gestured in Mark and Matthew's direction as he continued. "We've been discussing what's next for you, and we all agree that you might be ready to handle your own division."

Excitement pulled at Luke's expression. "Might?" the young man questioned, looking from one sibling to the other.

"Time will tell," John said, shrugging his broad shoulders.

A look of confusion washed over Luke's expression. "So, what does that mean?"

John leaned forward, his clasped hands moving from his lap to the conference tabletop. "It means that you are now solely responsible for the West End rejuvenation project."

Matthew nodded. "We will support whatever you want to do as long as you stay within the parameters dictated by the town council."

Mark interjected. "And please, don't irritate the mayor. We need him on our side."

John continued. "The details of the budget and the town council's criteria are all there. From start to finish you have exactly two years to get this project completed. Right now, you have eight weeks to pull your team together. I need you to give us your assessment of the property acquisitions, any revisions to the original proposal and budget and a detailed timeline. Any questions?"

"What's the budget?"

"One hundred million dollars, and not a penny more. Do you think you can handle it?" John answered.

Luke nodded, grinning broadly. "I welcome the challenge."

Matthew clasped his hands together on top of the table. "We hope so, baby brother. This one's a big deal. This rejuvenation project will be a coup for the city of Dallas and Stallion Enterprises' reputation. We're putting a lot of trust in you. If you really want to impress us, come in twenty million dollars under budget without compromising the integrity of the project."

Luke came to his feet, extending a large hand toward John. "You won't be disappointed," he said as he shook his brother's hand, his broad smile warming his dark face. "Thank you for the trust."

John nodded. "Just remember, if you need help, don't be too proud to let someone know. The only stupid question is the one you don't ask."

Pure adrenaline fueled Luke Stallion's ride from the corporate offices of Stallion Enterprises' luxury high-rise to the deteriorating Oak Cliff neighborhood the family was intent on revitalizing. It was a typical inner-city, working-class neighborhood renowned for its booming atmosphere back in the 1950s and 60s. Time had painted a new but not improved façade over the landscape despite the efforts of many grassroots and church organizations working to bring the community back to its original glow. The Stallions were hoping to do their part to inject some much-needed energy back into the area.

Parking his Mercedes coupe on the street, the young

man exited the vehicle, set the lock and alarm, deposited six quarters into the meter and set out on foot to explore the strained area.

The first lesson his brother John had taught them all was to learn every single detail of any venture they were pursuing. The more knowledge gained, the better, inevitably preparing them for the unexpected. Even before graduating from high school, Luke had been allowed to follow behind his brothers as they'd pursued their many business acquisitions. Luke vividly remembered trailing on John's heels as his brother had inspected every one of the steel ships that would become the cornerstone of their shipping empire. Luke had just been fifteen years old, and at the age of twenty-four his big brother had been recognized as the youngest self-made billionaire CEO.

Luke recognized that he had some pretty big Texas boots to fill in order to reap half the success John had. The fact that Mark and Matthew had achieved just as much notoriety since joining the family business didn't make the challenges ahead of him any easier. He welcomed the opportunity to prove himself worthy of his brothers' trust and looked forward to using this project to garner some attention of his own. He sighed, pausing to study the empty storefronts and dilapidated buildings that landscaped the neighborhood.

His thoughts trailed back to the earlier banter between him and his siblings. He and Matthew joked good-naturedly about John and Mark marrying as quickly as they had. Both men had fallen head over heels in love before any of them had realized it. Although Luke professed to not being able to imagine himself falling in love and committing to any one woman, he had to admit that the idea had recently become especially appealing.

Luke liked the changes that had come over Mark

and John. They were both more relaxed and easygoing since they'd gotten married. Both of them reeked of pure contentment, seemingly enjoying fabulously full relationships. Luke loved to witness the attention the wives lavished upon them—both Mark's wife, Michelle, and Marah, John's wife, committed wholeheartedly to the men in their lives. Luke secretly wished that for himself.

Being young and single had its moments, Luke mused, but he was hardly determined to keep it that way. For the moment he considered bachelorhood only a game of time and one that he played well, but he wasn't interested in taking it to a championship. The carefree lifestyle and the many beautiful women that went along with it was one thing, but the emotional security and companionship John and Mark had attained definitely appeared more desirable.

Being a master of casual romance had begun to grow weary on his spirit, and Luke felt he was almost ready to just let it all go. His big brothers had taught him well, but they'd also shown him that moving on had its positives. As if to prove that thought, Luke couldn't help but admire an Asian beauty who was peeking out of the door of a small variety store on the corner. He winked an easy eye and tilted his head in greeting as she tossed him a wide smile of snow-white teeth.

But relationships aside, at this point in his young life, what Luke wanted more than anything else was to prove himself capable of running his own division. In that moment, that was far more important than any romantic commitment could begin to be.

An hour later Luke had managed to circle the twenty blocks twice, stopping periodically to speak with the residents and remaining shopkeepers to ask their opinion about their neighborhood. Many had eyed him warily but were eventually taken in by his boyish good looks and charismatic demeanor. His warm personality was captivating, drawing people to him, and Luke worked that to his advantage, inciting conversation out of the more wary personalities.

One of the senior citizens had pointed him in the direction of the local community center, a makeshift facility housed in an abandoned warehouse off Arkansas Avenue. The building was home to the youth and senior centers, the food bank and a temporary shelter for families displaced from their homes. Although maintenance and upkeep of the building were funded through the city's budget, there was barely enough money to keep the lights on. Infrequent donations from a few generous benefactors and volunteers helped to offset many of the expenses that would have closed the center's doors and sent many back into the streets to fend for themselves.

Luke stood at the bottom of the steps of the facility peering up at the glass doors that beckoned him inside. The old man who'd guided him to the entrance pointed with his left index finger, his right hand clutching a brown paper bag as if it were filled with gold. Luke nodded his gratitude.

"Thanks," he said, pressing a crisp twenty-dollar bill into the old man's wrinkled hand. "I appreciate the help."

The old guy threw him a toothless grin. "No problem! Like I told you, this here is the heart of Oak Cliff. If you want to know what this neighborhood needs, sonny boy, you'll find it here," the man exclaimed excitedly as he turned an about-face, his newly gotten gains waving between his fingers.

Luke smiled warmly, watching as the man disappeared out of sight. With one last glance over his shoulder he climbed the short span of stairs, pulled the glass doors open and stepped inside.

A rush of noise and the pungent scent of lemon disinfectant greeted him at the entrance. A large reception area with a massive counter that spanned the lengths of two walls sat at the room's center. The floor was a checkerboard of black-and-white linoleum, the covering worn thin from age. The walls were painted a vibrant sunshine-yellow, the bright color gleaming with energy. Select posters of beaming parents and children above messages of encouragement smiled down on them, the décor sparse but warming.

There were four children—three little girls and a small boy—playing in the center of the floor. The space around them was strewn with plastic blocks and Matchbox cars. A teenage girl sat watching from one of two wooden benches, her gaze moving back and forth between the noise of their childish banter and the paperback book that rested open in her lap.

The young woman glanced in the direction of the door that had closed loudly behind Luke. She met his curious stare with one of her own, her mouth slowly lifting into a friendly smile. Luke smiled back, lifting his hand in a slight wave. Before he could ask for assistance, the little boy let out a loud scream, calling out to everyone that could hear that there was a strange man in the lobby.

Chapter 2

"Mizz Joanne! Mizz Joanne! Some man out here! Come quick, Mizz Joanne!"

Joanne Lake shook her head from side to side as she heard her name being called again and again, Mrs. Stanton's baby boy screaming at the top of his lungs. No matter how often they told that child to use his inside voice when he was inside, little Bryson preferred saying everything loudly, and he always had much to say.

Before she could lift herself from her seat, the boy came storming through the office doors. He barely missed slamming his face into the corner of the desk as he came to an abrupt halt. Joanne winced as he narrowly avoided what could have been a very nasty accident.

"Some man out here, Mizz Joanne. We don't know him. He's strange," Bryson Stanton sputtered, words spilling out faster than he could catch them.

Joanne smiled, shaking her head as she admonished

him. "Bryson, stop yelling. And what did I tell you about running when you're inside the building here? You could have hit your head and taken an eye out!"

"But there's a man—"

"I heard you, and I'm coming," she said as the little boy clasped her fingers in the palm of his small hand and tugged anxiously, trying to pull her to her feet.

"You got to come now, Mizz Joanne! Quick! He's a stranger! Stranger danger!" Bryson exclaimed loudly, his outstretched arms waving excitedly to emphasize the urgency.

Moving from the space of the small office to the outside reception area, Joanne chuckled softly at the child's exuberance, sensing that things weren't nearly as pressing as he'd proclaimed.

And then she saw him, 286 pounds of pure delectable dark chocolate standing six feet tall in navy slacks, a white polo shirt and leather slip-ons. Joanne's eyes widened with curiosity and obvious interest as her gaze raced from the top of his neatly cropped haircut down to the tips of his very expensive shoes.

The handsome man was standing in conversation with Bryson's older sister, Brenda, the sixteen-year-old leering at the stranger as if he were a bowl of ice cream and she were a spoon. As Joanne eyed them, she was only slightly taken aback by the girl's brazen behavior. Brenda looked as if she were just a hair away from throwing herself into the man's lap. Joanne and Brenda had had more than their fair share of conversations about the appropriate way for a young woman to behave, and Brenda was clearly intent on doing the opposite of what she had been shown.

Shaking her head, Joanne cleared her throat, interrupting whatever conversation Miss Brenda imagined herself having with a man as fine as that one. And the dark stranger was surely one fine man.

"Brenda, would you take the kids back to the recreation room, please. I'll handle this," Joanne said firmly.

"But, Miss Joanne, me and him was just—"

The stern look Joanne gave the girl cut her words off before she could think to finish her sentence. Brenda rolled her eyes skyward, sucking her teeth in annoyance. Snatching her book from where it rested on the bench, she tossed Luke one last smile. As she turned, gesturing to the little ones who stood watching, she gave Joanne one last glare. Joanne raised her eyebrows in response.

When Brenda had herded the kids toward the space behind her, Joanne turned her attention to the dark stranger who was staring at her with a wide smile plastered on his chiseled face. "I'm sorry, sir, but unless you're a resident, the center is actually closed for the evening. Is there something I can do for you?"

Luke nodded slowly, suddenly at a loss for words. He hadn't been expecting to see such an exquisite woman come into the room. The stunning female was absolutely beautiful. Her warm smile was engaging, brightening her face with energy. She was a full-figured beauty with a deep copper complexion, a closely cropped hairstyle, and the most luscious, ready-to-be-kissed pout of any woman Luke had ever seen. The look she gave him sparked a wave of emotion that had his cheeks burning with warmth at the perverse thoughts that suddenly coursed through his mind.

Joanne repeated herself. "Excuse me, but I asked if there was something I can help you with?" she queried, a look of rising concern filling her dark brown eyes. "Sir, are you all right?"

Luke shook his head quickly from side to side. "Excuse

me. I'm sorry. My name is Luke, Luke Stallion, and I was just wondering if I could ask you a few questions. My company is acquiring some of the property in this area as part of the city's rejuvenation project, and I'm researching how we can best benefit the neighborhood." Luke finally extended a hand to shake hers. "One of your neighbors thought you might be able to help me." He flashed her a dimpled smile.

Joanne's gaze moved from the man's face down to his outstretched palm as her own hand was suddenly lost beneath the fingertips that clasped hers tightly. Her gaze moved back to his face, her breath suddenly caught in her chest as the heat of his touch surprised her. She pulled her hand from his, clasping it against her abdomen, as she tried to ignore a distinct rise of discomfort.

"It's a pleasure to meet you, Mr. Stallion. My name is Joanne Lake. I'm just one of the volunteers here. You probably want to talk to the center's director. His name is Daniel Manchuck, and he'll be back on Monday. I'm sure he'll be delighted to answer any questions you may have."

"I appreciate that, but I'd also like to know what you think, as well, Ms. Lake. I'm hoping to reach out to everyone in the neighborhood for their input."

Joanne raised a curious eyebrow. "That's interesting, Mr. Stallion. Most corporations couldn't care less what a community thinks about their business decisions. Why do you?" Joanne shifted her weight onto one full hip, her arms crossing over an ample chest.

"I beg to differ, Ms. Lake. I'd argue that most corporations care very much. Ultimately, unhappy customers could negatively impact a company's bottom line, and none of us wants to see that happen."

"Heaven forbid your company's bottom line isn't

favorable," Joanne said, a hint of cynicism rising in her voice.

A slow smile pulled at Luke's full lips. "Most companies just want to know that their efforts are received favorably. Ultimately, Stallion Enterprises wants to know that what we do benefits everyone in the long run."

"I'm sure," Joanne said, her tone everything but convinced.

Luke's eyes roamed around the room, taking in the view of the space that surrounded him. "This is some facility you have here," he said, changing the direction of their conversation. "I'm impressed."

Joanne eyed him warily before responding, her eyes following where his eyes led. "We're very proud of the center. Everyone involved here is totally dedicated to making things better for the families that utilize our services."

Luke nodded. "I know you're closed, but would you consider giving me a quick tour?" he asked sweetly.

Joanne paused for a brief moment. Had it been anyone else, she would have politely refused, but there was something about the man that made her suddenly respond with a resounding yes. "I'd love to, Mr. Stallion."

Luke grinned widely, his dimples blossoming full in his cheeks. "Please, call me Luke. My father was Mr. Stallion."

The beautiful woman grinned back, her head bowing slightly in acknowledgment. "It's a pleasure to meet you, Luke. Call me Joanne."

For exactly two hours, thirty-seven minutes and twelve seconds Joanne had guided Luke Stallion from one end of the community center to the other. They'd toured the recreation room where kids were doing their homework and playing board games, had strolled easily through the kitchen as the last free meal was being served and had even walked through the men's housing unit, where the lucky few were preparing themselves to bed down on a cot for the night.

Luke had asked question after question about the center's policies and procedures, picking Joanne's brains for all the information he could about them and the neighborhood. The woman had been impressed when he'd stopped to offer one of the young men help with his calculus homework. Afterward, the two guys had joined in a quick pickup game on the basketball court. She'd been awed speechless when Luke had taken off his shirt, flexing his muscles as he'd dropped ball after ball into the hoop.

His nicely toned physique had been startling. His sturdy neck melded down to broad, sculptured shoulders, beefy biceps and bulging forearms. His pecs were so defined that they cast a shadow on his perfectly defined abdomen. The V shape of his torso ended at the waistband of his slacks. His thighs bulged as if barely contained. His pants creased from the hips to a prominent bulge in the front. Joanne had to fight not to stare, wondering what might be hidden beneath the covering of his slacks.

The man's rock-hard build had only been outdone by his engaging eyes and the generous smile that had commanded her full attention. The prominent businessman had made quite an impression on the many residents availing themselves of the center's services. The impact he'd had on Joanne had been just as engaging.

Joanne heaved a deep sigh as she closed her apartment door behind her, then tossed her purse and keys onto the glass tabletop in the foyer of her home. Silence greeted her, the quiet in her house kissing her hello. *I really should get myself a pet,* she thought, more aware than ever before that there was no companion, male or otherwise, to welcome her home.

Moving from the entrance into the home's living space, Joanne dropped down into an upholstered wing chair and kicked off her low heels. She lifted her feet onto the matching ottoman, wiggling her toes in front of her. Her day had been long, starting before six that morning with an hour of Pilates to stretch her muscles. After a quick shower and a granola bar breakfast, she'd had meetings with her fabric designer, two potential buyers for her new dress line and the staff of seamstresses who sewed for her design company, Lake Fashions. She'd conducted more business before her salad-and-sandwich lunch than some folks did in a whole day.

Her entire afternoon had been devoted to the community center and the mountain of paperwork that had needed attention there, and now she had a full night of designing ahead of her. Her time with Luke Stallion had put her a few hours behind schedule, but it had been a few hours that had been well wasted.

Luke Stallion. Joanne was suddenly aware that she was grinning broadly at the very thought of the handsome man. The image of him was still very vivid in her mind's eye. The staggering looks he'd given her had ignited a fiery flood of emotions through her bloodstream, leaving her heated with desire she'd not experienced in a very long time. She suddenly shuddered at the intense feelings sweeping through her.

She hadn't told him so, but she was acutely aware of who the Stallion brothers were, having met the oldest brother, John, at a cotillion fundraiser many years back. The man had been exceptionally charming, catching the attention of every single female searching for love within a hundred-mile radius of Dallas.

Joanne had only been seventeen at the time, but it had been more than evident that the eldest Stallion had been something special. Now, having met the younger brother, Joanne would firmly attest that good looks and that dynamic charm ran strong through the family's bloodline. John had just been the tip of the dessert tray. Luke was clearly the icing *and* the cake.

Joanne remembered reading in the society page that John and another brother had both married, taking themselves off everyone's potential husband list. Thinking about Luke and the brief time they'd just shared together, she couldn't help but hope that his personal relationship status might be single and available.

Chapter 3

Luke heard them before he saw them, hushed giggles and laughter coming from the darkened room. He shook his head slowly as he made his way into the kitchen, switching on the room's bright lights as he did. He didn't bother to look in the direction from where all the noise was coming. He knew clearly what he would or wouldn't see, having interrupted his brother and new sister-in-law more times than he cared to count. It amazed him that the two couldn't be in the same room together for five minutes before they were wrapped around each other like bark on a cedar elm tree.

Luke moved to the refrigerator, opening the stainless-steel door to peer inside the cold cavity. His name was written on a yellow sticky note affixed to a large plate of food wrapped in aluminum foil. Lifting up the foil edge he peered inside, fried chicken and macaroni and cheese awaiting his attention.

"Who fried chicken?" Luke asked, addressing the couple cuddled against the pantry door.

"You know the only cooking I do is takeout," Michelle said with a soft chuckle. "Engines are my specialty. I don't do cakes."

"Aunt Juanita was here," Mark responded, his answer muffled in his wife's neck.

Michelle giggled softly as she nuzzled her husband back.

"They have hotel rooms for that kind of nonsense," Luke said nonchalantly, moving himself and his plate from the refrigerator to the microwave oven. "You two should give it a try sometime."

Mark laughed loudly as Michelle leaned her back against his chest, her husband's arms wrapping warmly around her. The two of them turned to stare at the younger man. "Luke's got jokes. My little brother thinks he's funny!"

Luke shrugged, a wry smile pulling at his mouth. "Your little brother doesn't want to keep walking in on the two of you making out all over the house like you don't know what a bed is for. It's creepy!" Luke cringed, skewing his face like a five-year-old might. "And it's starting to seriously warp my psyche."

Michelle laughed. "No date tonight, Luke?"

Luke crossed his arms over his chest as he leaned back against the center island. "Rub it in, why don't you. Just add salt to my wound. I don't have a date, and you two keep going at it like rabbits."

Michelle moved to Luke's side, rubbing the palm of her hand against his forearm. "You should talk to Eden and Marah. I'm sure those two would be thrilled to fix you up with someone."

Luke rolled his eyes. "Heaven help me. I don't know which is scarier—those two playing matchmaker or me constantly walking in on you and him naked." Luke cringed.

Michelle gave him a light punch to his shoulder, her cheeks heating with color. "You were supposed to be gone that night. You should have warned us."

"No, you should have warned me," Luke said with a hearty laugh. "I'm so scarred that I'm ready to go spill my guts to Oprah." He pulled his freshly heated meal from the microwave oven, inhaling the decadent aroma rising from the plate.

"So, do you have any plans for tonight?" Mark asked.

Luke chuckled, pulling a spoonful of macaroni to his mouth. "Don't act like you're interested in my plans, Mark. I'll be out of your way in a few minutes. Then you two can go back to doing what you were doing."

"What?" Mark feigned innocence, pretending to be hurt by his brother's insinuation. "You act like I don't have your best interests at heart."

Luke laughed. "I am not stupid, big brother. The only thing you're interested in right now is Mitch." His sister-in-law's childhood nickname rolled off his tongue as he met her amused gaze. "Ain't that right, Mrs. Stallion?"

Michelle laughed with him, moving back to her husband's side. "You two need to stop." She leaned up to kiss Mark's mouth. "But since you brought the subject up, we'll just head upstairs and get out of your way," she said, eyeing her husband suggestively.

Mark broke out into a full grin, following behind Michelle as she pulled him from where he stood and headed in the direction of the door. Behind them Luke rolled his eyes skyward, the trio still sharing a warm laugh with each other as the couple made their exit.

Watching them, Luke couldn't help but smile. He'd been responsible for introducing his brother to one of his dearest friends. The wild child of the family, Mark had been headed out on one of his cross-country jaunts to the annual black bike festival in Myrtle Beach, South Carolina. Luke had recommended Michelle, the best mechanic he knew, to get his brother's bike travel-ready. Before anyone knew what had happened, Michelle had tamed the once wild Stallion and Mark had fallen in love with a woman who was headstrong and beautiful.

Minutes later the house was quiet, only the sound of the large grandfather clock in the center hall ticking in the background. As Luke sat finishing his evening meal, he couldn't stop himself from thinking about the woman he'd met earlier.

With her enigmatic personality, Joanne Lake had lit up the room, commanding his full and undivided attention. Luke couldn't remember the last time he'd met a woman with the wealth of confidence Joanne had exuded. Joanne could easily have been the poster child for women who were not a size 6 but loved every curve and dip of their bodies. With her understated style and poise, she'd tempted every one of his senses, and he found himself completely intrigued by her.

Luke's hand tightened around the glass of tart lemonade he'd been drinking. He was thinking about the easy lift to Joanne's mouth, her gentle smile sending waves of heat through every nerve ending in his body. When she'd laughed, the sensuous sound had been like lighter fluid tossed on an already raging flame. The wealth of it had left him breathless. Luke shifted in his seat, the pressure building deep inside of him threatening to take full control of his senses.

Luke sensed that given some time he and Joanne could become fast friends. He imagined that having a woman like her for a friend wouldn't be a bad thing at all. After all, he had many female friends. Most were just casual companions that he would spend some recreational time with. Rarely did it have anything to do with any serious boyfriend-girlfriend expectations. Luke imagined that he would enjoy just hanging out with Joanne, the two of them enjoying the camaraderie of each other's company, neither having any expectations whatsoever.

And then again, he thought, mulling over the details of their afternoon one more time, Joanne's self-confidence had been sexy as hell, seriously inciting some testosterone-fueled male curiosity. As images of her shot through his mind, an unexpected quiver of heat suddenly radiated through his groin. Maybe having Joanne for a friend might actually become more of a problem than not, he mused.

For a brief second, before they'd parted company, he had thought of asking her to dinner. And then he'd hesitated, unable to form a complete thought about where, what or when. The moment had been interrupted as Joanne had been called away to the telephone, leaving him tongue-tied while another volunteer showed him to the exit door. Standing on the sidewalk outside the center, the first waves of nightfall beginning to sweep dark and full across the sky had found him flustered, his own confidence suddenly challenged.

Luke pushed his empty plate away from him, shaking his head as he replayed the experience over and over again in his head. The two could hardly become friends if he did that again.

The next time, he thought suddenly, he would take full advantage of any opportunity he had to spend time with Ms. Lake and get to know her better. And he was determined that there would definitely be another opportunity. He'd be better prepared when that moment took place. Better prepared to discover all he could about Ms. Lake and hopefully intrigue her enough to want to know more about him. Fast friends and a solid friendship needed to start somewhere.

Chapter 4

On Monday morning, one whole hour before the community center's doors were officially unlocked for the day, Luke sat outside on the steps in wait. He was anxious to speak with the center's director and even more excited with the prospect of seeing Joanne again. Joanne Lake had been on his mind all weekend, thoughts of the woman sneaking in when he least expected them. He'd shrugged it off at first, and then she'd snuck into his dreams, disrupting his sleep, and his curiosity had kicked into overdrive.

Stopping by his office first to handle some necessary paperwork, his morning had started bright and early. As he sat watching children being hurried off to school and parents rushing to work, he was grateful for the brief respite of quiet to collect his thoughts and formulate a game plan for the rest of his day.

Both John and Matthew had beat him to the office that morning, the two men huddled together in deep discussion when Luke had entered the luxury office space. The duo had reiterated the importance of the rejuvenation project, and Luke had to admit that he was already feeling some pressure. Add to that his sudden preoccupation with a woman he'd only met briefly and he knew he had to have a solid course of action to follow before he lost control of both situations. John and Matthew both had reminded him that a man with distractions was a man who made mistakes. Luke didn't have room for any mistakes, and he had no intentions of losing control.

His thoughts were suddenly interrupted, a soft voice murmuring behind him.

"Hey, money! What 'chu doin' here?"

Luke turned to see the young woman from his previous visit eyeing him eagerly. His full lips bent into an easy smile. "Good morning. It's Brenda, right?"

She nodded enthusiastically, her gaze sweeping over the denim jeans, denim shirt and bright white sneakers that he was dressed in. "So, you come back to see me?" she asked coyly, fingering the ribbon that held her shirt closed at her neck.

Luke chuckled. "I came to see Ms. Lake."

Brenda rolled her eyes and scowled. "What 'chu want her fo'?"

"It's business," Luke responded, rising to his feet and taking a step back as Brenda eased herself closer to him. "So, are you headed off to school?"

The girl scowled, shrugging her narrow shoulders skyward. "I guess. You gon' be here when I get back?" she asked, her tone hopeful.

"Probably not," Luke answered, crossing his arms over his chest. "But you have a good day, okay?"

The girl angled her head. "Come back soon, you hear!" she exclaimed as she walked away, moving to join a gathering of teens who were watching them closely. She turned, tossing him a brash wink. "I know Miss Lake can't handle a man like you. But I'll be here if you want some real fun!"

Brenda laughed, her friends snickering with her, and Luke suddenly felt like he was the punch line at the end of a very bad joke. He frowned, his mood shifting ever so slightly. "Goodbye, Brenda," he said, no hint of playfulness in his tone.

Joanne was standing inside the center's reception area when Luke entered the building. His grin was full and wide, his excitement shining in his eyes when he saw her. "Good morning, Ms. Lake," he said, tipping his head in greeting.

"Good morning, Mr. Stallion," Joanne greeted, her own excitement spilling over in her voice.

"We're being formal with each other again, Ms. Lake. I thought we'd gotten past all that," Luke said teasingly as he leaned his elbows on the counter.

"You started it."

Luke laughed. "I guess I did. Joanne."

She tilted her head. "Luke," she said, responding with his first name. "So, what brings you back here this morning?"

"I'm still searching for information. I was hoping to meet with your director, of course, and talk to more of your clients."

Joanne nodded her head. "Well, Daniel's not here yet, but we expect him shortly."

Luke nodded, his eyes flitting back and forth across her beautiful face. "So, tell me again, what is it that you do here?"

The woman smiled. "Do you suffer from short-term

memory problems, Luke? You don't seem like a man who'd forget a detail like that so quickly."

Luke chuckled. "I didn't. I was just making conversation." The coy look she gave him sent a shiver up and down his spine.

Joanne studied him momentarily, her gaze racing from the top of his head down to his feet. The man's stare was unnerving, causing a rise of perspiration to bead across her brow and in the deep valley between her breasts. She fanned a hand before her face, turning quickly to keep him from seeing the expression that crossed it.

"You're welcome to sit and wait, Mr. Stallion. Daniel shouldn't be much longer."

"Will you wait with me?" Luke asked, his tone hopeful. "We could…just…talk," he said, suddenly stammering.

Joanne shook her head, still refusing to meet his gaze. "I'm sorry. I have to go head downtown to help some of our clients arrange payment plans for their utility bills." She tossed him a quick glance over her shoulder. He was still looking at her intently. Joanne spun back around to face him. "Perhaps another time," she said as she took a deep inhale of air and held it.

"I'll hold you to that," Luke answered, his deep tone promising. "So, perhaps when you get back?"

Joanne paused, warm breath seeping slowly past her lips. "I may be a while. You'll probably be gone by the time I get back."

Luke tossed her a quick wink. "Don't count on it," he said huskily. Their eyes met and held for a minute until Joanne broke the connection, turning away from him.

Crossing the room toward the front door, Joanne was acutely aware of him watching her side-to-side sashay with much appreciation. A slight smile pulled at her mouth as she fought to contain the rising anxiety, wanting to pretend not to notice. Behind her, Luke was still staring, unable to take his eyes off her.

Hours later when Joanne walked back through the doors of the center, Luke and Daniel Manchuck, the center's director, were knee deep in conversation. Joanne peeked into the office where the two men sat, curious about the hearty laughter that echoed down the corridor toward the reception area. The two men sat on opposite sides of an old metal desk, legs and arms crossed comfortably in front of them. Conversation flowed between them like they'd been friends since forever. A leather portfolio sat in Luke's lap, his large hand wrapped easily around an ink pen as he jotted notes into the margins of a note pad. He was firing questions at the other man as fast as they could be answered, clearly interested in what they were discussing.

The man was drop-dead gorgeous, Joanne thought, admiring the casual styling of his attire. Even with him sitting, it was evident that Luke Stallion was one well-built specimen of maleness. Having been given a sneak peek at what lay beneath his wardrobe only served to fuel some wicked thoughts in the woman's mind. She closed her eyes briefly, imagining what it might be like to draw her palms across his broad chest and caress the dark chocolate lines of his sculpted back. Joanne gasped softly, her eyes opening quickly to see if anyone had seen her. The two men were still lost in conversation as she resumed staring. Joanne stood eyeing him for some time before either realized she was there.

As he spun around in his chair, Dan's gaze swept across the doorway. He suddenly took note of her quietly standing in the entrance. Waving his hand in her direction, he gave her a bright smile. "Hey, Joanne! We didn't see you standing there."

Luke looked up just as Joanne lifted her hand in greeting, calling out both their names. "Gentlemen, good afternoon. I didn't want to interrupt. You two looked busy." A brilliant smile flooded her face. "It's good to see you again, Luke," she said directing that smile in his direction.

As if startled, Luke jumped to his feet, spilling half his papers onto the floor as he knocked over the chair behind him. A wave of heat flushed his dark face as he struggled to regain his composure. "Hi," Luke finally managed to mutter. He knelt down to scoop up the documents that had dropped out of his hands, managing only to drop the balance of them instead.

Joanne laughed out loud at the sight of him looking so bewildered and nervous. "It's just a hello," she said giggling softly as she moved to help him pick up his papers.

Only slightly embarrassed, Luke laughed with her. "Not too smooth, huh?" he said, chuckling deeply.

Joanne's eyes shimmered with amusement. "No. Not smooth at all." She handed him his documents, her hand brushing gently against his as she did.

There was no mistaking the sudden current of electricity that passed between them, both pulling back as if they'd been burned. Surprised, Joanne stood quickly, taking a step away from him. Her own cheeks were suddenly bright with color.

Heat warmed Luke's cheeks as well as he gestured with the papers in his hand. "Thank you," he said, moving to pick up the chair he'd been occupying. A wide grin spread from ear to ear. "Dan, do you think you can help a brother out here?" he said with a deep chuckle.

"There is no saving you from that smooth move, guy," Dan said, humor washing over his expression. He looked from one to the other. "Since you two are already acquainted, I'll dispense with the introductions and get right to business. Joanne, why don't you come take a seat. We were just discussing some of the new programs you were hoping to initiate here. Luke has some great ideas, as well."

"Really?" Joanne said, her expression curious as she moved to sit down.

Luke nodded. "I was just telling Dan about Briscoe Ranch. We've initiated some great community programs for students to come out and work with the horses. I think a joint program between our two organizations might be beneficial to the kids here."

Joanne nodded her head as she moved to take the seat beside him. She didn't miss the stare Luke gave her, his gaze sweeping from her head down to her toes and back again. She was glad for her wardrobe choice that morning, having selected one of her own designs. The dress was a form-fitting wrap in a summer floral that accentuated her full bust line and fuller rear end. The dress draped her nicely, highlighting everything that was feminine about her. She felt herself smiling foolishly as she took in the appreciation that washed over her from Luke's deep gaze.

Luke couldn't stop himself from staring. She was even more beautiful than he remembered. Everything about her was screaming out for his attention, and she had it, full and undivided. Luke was totally enthralled, feeling as if someone or something had blindsided him with some sort of magic charm. The feelings were unsettling, like nothing he'd ever experienced before and definitely nothing his big brothers had warned him about. The sound of his name suddenly pulled him back into the moment.

"Luke?"

"I'm sorry. I lost my train of thought," Luke said, shaking his head slightly. "Where were we?"

Joanne raised a curious eyebrow. "I asked what Stallion Enterprises would be gaining from any venture between us."

Luke nodded. "The knowledge that we are serving people in need."

Dan interrupted. "Before I forget," he said extending his hand and a small slip of paper toward Joanne. "Luke has made a very nice donation to the center. I'd appreciate it if you'd pass this on to accounting for me. I have a meeting downtown in ten minutes about those permits, and I know I'll forget it," he said, glancing down at the watch on his wrist.

Joanne reached for the personal check being passed to her. As she did she cut her eye in Luke's direction. He was watching her intently. Daniel moved from behind his desk toward the door.

"Luke, I hate to rush off, but I leave you in very capable hands. It was a pleasure meeting you. I look forward to us talking more."

Luke shook the hand that had been extended toward him. "The pleasure was all mine, Dan. How about we do lunch next week?"

Dan pointed a finger in Luke's direction. "I'll buy." He turned toward Joanne, leaning as he wrapped an arm around her shoulder in a friendly embrace. "Thanks, Joanne. I'll call you later and let you know how we made out."

"Good luck," Joanne exclaimed as Dan rushed out the door.

As quickly as he was out of sight, silence spread like wildfire in the space between Luke and Joanne. She looked down to the check in her hand, her eyes widening in surprise as she surveyed the amount. "This is quite generous of you," she said, lifting her gaze to meet his.

Luke smiled. "It's the least I can do. The center clearly needs all the help it can get."

Joanne rose from her seat, moving to the other side of the desk to sit in the space Dan had just occupied. Her expression was suddenly serious as she fell into deep thought. Luke sensed that Joanne wasn't wildly happy about his donation.

"Is something wrong?" he asked, noting the furrows that creased her forehead.

Joanne shrugged, her shoulders lifting toward the wide hoop earrings that adorned her ears. "The center can use as much money as it can get, so I don't want to sound unappreciative, but have you ever considered giving more?"

"More than that?" Luke queried, not quite understanding her question.

"More than money."

"I'm not sure I understand."

"There are boys and young men here who don't have a male figure in their lives to emulate and look up to. The center is always looking for mentors. Have you considered donating your time, as well?"

Luke hesitated, suddenly thrown by her tone and the direction the conversation had taken. "Well, I—" Luke started.

Joanne interjected before he could finish his thought. "I didn't think so. Money is always the answer for you, isn't it? As long as you can pay for it, then the problem is solved, right?" she said. Her tone was cutting.

Luke bristled. "No, not at all. I have no problems doing what I can when I can."

Joanne nodded, waving a hand dismissively. "I'm sure. And please, I'm really not trying to be critical. It's just that I've met your type before."

Luke eyed her curiously, leaning forward in his seat. "And just what is my type?"

"Wealthy men who think flashing that wealth absolves them of any personal responsibility to the social ills that plague our society. Men more concerned with their bank accounts than with their neighbor."

Luke rolled his eyes. "Give me a break. Wealth by no means absolves any of us from anything. Yes, I have money and my financial security enables me to do things other people can't do. But since it is my money to spend as I see fit, then there should only be a problem with that if what I am spending my money on is doing other people more harm than good. And even then that's debatable."

"What about getting your hands dirty every now and then? What about getting down in the trenches and working with the poor and underprivileged one-on-one? Have you ever thought about doing that?"

"As a matter of fact, I have. I have volunteered many times before, Ms. Lake, as time and opportunity have allowed me to. But since you don't know me, you wouldn't know that, would you? And for a woman who's not trying to be critical, you're sure doing one heck of a job. You're also passing judgment without being informed." Luke crossed his arms over his chest, leaning back in his seat as he continued to stare her down.

A flash of something Joanne didn't recognize gripped her nerves, a wealth of emotion rising without warning. The man was eyeing her so intensely that it felt like he could see straight through her. She felt exposed and vulnerable, and she didn't like it one bit.

She took a deep breath, fighting to collect her thoughts. "My apologies," she said finally, contrition filling her face, "and perhaps I was, but I've encountered too many wealthy people who care right up until the check clears the bank, and then they forget all about the people they were supposed to be helping until the next time they need a tax deduction. Children can go hungry between those deposits."

She paused, her gaze locking with his. "So now that you've written your check, Mr. Stallion, what next? What will the children and their families have to look forward to after you and your money sweep in to make the neighborhood a better place for all the poor people and then you disappear? Because that's how this is going to work, isn't it? You've written your check and now you're going to disappear?"

Luke took a deep inhale of air, filling his lungs and blowing it slowly past his full lips. He pushed himself up and out of his seat, leaning over the desk on his forearms, his eyes meeting hers evenly. He smiled deeply, the gesture pocketing full dimples in his dark cheeks. "Joanne Lake, I'm not going anywhere, so you can take my check, and that promise, straight to the bank."

Chapter 5

"You like this man!"

Joanne groaned loudly as her best friend, Marley Brooks, hovered above her.

Marley stood with her hands on her narrow hips, her braided extensions swaying against her shoulders. "You like this man and so you went right on the attack. Now what kind of sense did that make?"

"I did not attack him!" Joanne exclaimed, dropping her head back to the tabletop and banging her forehead against it. "I can't believe that I attacked him like that!"

Joanne was suddenly rattled. It galled her to admit that her friend was right. The entire time she'd been in the man's company all she could think about was kissing him. His full lips had been inviting, begging her to meet his mouth with her own, and even in their disagreement, Joanne hadn't been able to contain the rise of desire that had consumed her. The only way she knew to rid herself of her wanting had been to pretend he wasn't a man she could imagine herself being with. All she could think to do was to attack the one thing about him that she knew the two had in common—their wealth.

Marley laughed, her gaze moving to the man standing behind the counter of the coffee shop. "Rick, we need two caramel frappucinos with extra caramel, please."

The man named Rick nodded his head, giving her a thumbs-up as Marley dropped down into the seat beside her friend.

"So, is he as cute as I've heard?" she asked excitedly.

Joanne groaned again. "Cuter," she said, still not bothering to look up. "And I made a complete idiot out of myself."

Marley shrugged. "You always do. Why do you always have a problem with the rich boys? We both know you're not looking for any unemployed Joe still living with his mother."

Joanne sat herself upright, meeting the other woman's gaze. "You say that like all I do is judge a man by how much money he makes."

"If the shoe fits…"

Joanne rolled her eyes skyward. "Oh, please…"

Their conversation was interrupted as Rick dropped the two iced drinks onto the table in front of them. He paused, giving Marley an annoyed look. Marley gave him one back.

"I swear, Rick, just give me five more minutes. I do get a break!"

Grunting his response, Rick moved back to his station, his attention drawn to a customer in need of a coffee fix.

Marley leaned back in her seat, crossing her arms over her chest. "So, what happened next?"

"Nothing. He stood up, put his papers back into his briefcase, winked at me and walked out of the room."

"So, do you think he'll really come back?"

Joanne nodded. "Before I left they told me that he'd been put on the volunteer schedule for the next three weeks. I'll see him again tomorrow."

"Sounds like boyfriend might like you back," Marley said with a soft giggle.

"It's not like that. He's just volunteering."

"You kill me. One minute you want him volunteering and then when he does, you sound like it's the end of the world."

"Oh, like he's a guy I really want to see after he called me judgmental."

"And you telling him his giving spirit wasn't really so giving might not make him want to jump your bones anytime soon, either."

"What are you trying to say?"

"I'm saying you've got some issues, my friend, and those issues aren't going to help you in your search for a man. See a shrink and get yourself fixed."

Joanne dropped her head back down to the table. "Go back to work, Marley. I don't know why I told you."

Marley giggled. "Because I'm your best friend and you tell me everything!" She sipped her drink before continuing. "So, if you're really not interested in Mr. Stallion, will you introduce him to me? I promise I won't run him, or his money, off."

Joanne lifted her eyes to glare at her friend. "Marley, bite me!"

Still laughing, Marley stood back up, grabbing her beverage as she moved toward the back of the service counter. "Yep, you do like that man!"

* * *

When Luke poked his head into Matthew's office, his brother was in deep concentration over a stack of legal documents. He was almost reluctant to disturb him, but he needed some advice. He knocked, raising his hand in a quick wave as Matthew lifted his eyes to see who was there.

"Hey, Luke, what's up?"

"Do you have a minute? I could use a friend."

Matthew dropped his ballpoint pen to the desktop. "For you, little brother, I have two minutes. Come on in and close the door." Pushing himself away from the large mahogany desk, Matthew came to his feet. He moved to the other side of the room, gesturing for Luke to join him in the upholstered chairs that sat around a small conference table.

"So, what's up?"

Luke took a deep breath, suddenly nervous. It wasn't like this was the first time he'd had to turn to one of his kin for advice about women, but this wasn't just any woman.

Matthew eyed his baby brother curiously, the young man's brow creased in thought. "Are you okay?"

Luke met the man's gaze, his head bobbing up and down against his neck. "Yeah, I'm fine. It's just that…you see…well, there's this woman—"

"She's not pregnant, is she?" Matthew asked, concern flooding his face.

"No, nothing like that," he replied with a nervous chuckle. "I think I could deal with that."

"No time soon I hope because that truly is not the kind of trouble you need right now."

"Really, Matthew, that's not my problem. You see, I met this woman. She volunteers down at the community center and…" Luke paused, suddenly not sure what the problem was.

"Let me back up," he said, changing gears. "Do you think we're selfish? I mean, do you think we take our wealth for granted? This woman accused me of just tossing my money around without regard for people who are in serious need, and I have to tell you, it grated a nerve."

"What was she saying, that you don't give enough money away?"

"She thinks I need to be volunteering more of my time instead of giving my money away."

"That's different."

Luke shrugged. "Do I give off the impression that I'm more about our money than anything else?"

Matthew sank back into the sofa, a slight smile pulling at his mouth. "Before I answer that, why are you so concerned about what this woman thinks about you? John always told us that what we thought about ourselves was more important than anything. If you know in your own heart that what you're doing is right, then what does it matter what she thinks? Why is it bothering you so much?"

"Because she…" Luke paused, searching for the right words to convey what he was feeling. He suddenly found himself questioning exactly what that was. He met his brother's stare, his expression pensive.

Matthew chuckled. "If I'm not mistaken, this woman has your nose wide open!"

"What?"

"Look at you. Are you falling for this girl?"

Luke stood up, moving from his chair to the window, shaking his head vehemently. "No!" he exclaimed, almost shouting the word. "It's not like that." He peered through the blinds to the landscape outside. "I don't really know her yet. She just…well…"

Matthew laughed out loud. "If you say so," he said, clearly unconvinced. "Who is she?"

Luke shook his head, a shy smirk filling his face. "Her name is Joanne. Joanne Lake. That's really all I know about her."

"Is she cute?"

Luke grinned broadly, moving back to sit in his chair. He leaned forward, excitement blanketing his expression. "Brother, the woman is too fine! She is deliciously thick with curves that make a man weak in the knees." He blew warm breath past his full lips, shaking his head as memories of Joanne flashed through his mind. A rush of heat suddenly ran south, moving him to cross his right leg over his left, his hands falling casually into his lap as he leaned back.

"Well, she must be something special for you to be so interested."

Luke returned his brother's stare. He nodded slowly. "Yeah, I think she is."

Matthew rose from his own seat and moved to Luke's side, patting a broad hand against the younger man's shoulder. "Then get to know her and let her get to know you. You're a pretty special guy yourself. If it works between the two of you, then you won't have to worry about what she thinks about the money. It won't matter to her one way or the other."

Luke nodded. "Thanks." He took a deep breath before continuing. "Do you think about getting married, Matthew? I mean, since John and Mark both tied the knot, do you ever think about it?"

Matthew smirked, then shrugged his shoulders. "Actually I try not to, little brother. I mean, why ruin a good thing? Look, you're still young and idealistic. Committing yourself to a serious relationship should be the least of your concerns. You have all the time in the world to be worrying about that grown-up endeavor. For now, just enjoy yourself."

Before Luke could reply, the office intercom sounded from Matthew's desk, his secretary's voice rising from the microphoned box.

"Mr. Stallion?"

"Yes, Carol?"

"Vanessa Long is holding on line two for you. I told her you weren't taking calls, but she insisted that you would take hers. She says it's important."

Luke raised a curious eyebrow. Vanessa Long was an old family friend by virtue of her long-time friendship with their brother Mark. There had been a time when the whole family had been certain that Mark and Vanessa would end up in wedded bliss, but shortly after high school Vanessa had come out of the closet, announcing her preference for women. Mark's very best friend had suddenly become his very best lesbian friend.

There was nothing unusual about Vanessa calling the office or their home, but usually she was calling Mark. Rarely did Vanessa call any of the others. If she spoke to any of them it was usually by default, Mark being unavailable. Luke couldn't help but notice the look that crossed Matthew's face, his brother suddenly seeming anxious. He couldn't keep himself from prying. "What's Vanessa calling about?" Luke asked, curiosity flooding his face.

Matthew shrugged, ignoring his brother's question. "Carol, tell her I'm in a meeting with Luke and I'll call her back as soon as we're free, please."

"Yes, sir."

The intercom's soft hum quieted as the woman in the

exterior office severed the connection. Matthew turned his attention back to his brother.

"And to answer your first questions, yes, I do think you sometimes take your wealth for granted. But that's because you don't have any memories of when we didn't have money, not like the rest of us do. It's all you know. Plus John and Mark spoiled you. You've always had everything you needed and most things you wanted.

"But no, you are not selfish. Don't let anyone tell you otherwise. Now, I have a ton of work to get through, and I'm sure you have a long list to complete yourself. I'll see you at the house later," Matthew said, dismissing him.

Luke smiled as his brother moved back to his desk and sat down. Matthew was good, but he wasn't that good. He'd evaded Luke's question, but curiosity was a strange beast, always intruding where it was least wanted. The younger man persisted. "So, you're not going to answer my last question?"

Matthew focused his gaze on the pile of papers atop his desk, feigning interest in the stack of manila folders. "What question was that?"

"What's Vanessa calling *you* for?"

Matthew looked up, tossing his brother an easy smile. "I guess once you leave I'll be able to call her back and find out, won't I?"

Luke laughed, heading toward the door, his brother's smug expression following him out the exit.

Chapter 6

Between lending a hand in the recreational room with the younger kids, mentoring their older siblings with homework projects, driving senior citizens to doctor's appointments and helping parents navigate government aid and applications, Luke spent a lot of time asking questions and familiarizing himself with the issues that were relevant to the neighborhood. And for each question he asked about what was needed and what was wanted, he was asking two questions about Joanne.

Had Joanne been even remotely aware that so many people were discussing her, Luke knew it would have been a problem. He lifted his gaze to stare at her across the room, watching as she sat in discussion with a group of teen girls about their college options.

Since their last extended conversation, when Joanne had questioned his moral principles, she seemed to be avoiding him, or at least avoiding any in-depth conversations with him. Initially, Luke hadn't been sure how to take her aloofness, but he was still intrigued. The woman absolutely fascinated him.

Clearly, Joanne had issues with his wealth. Luke couldn't help but wonder if it was because her own history had been so substantially modest. If what everyone said about her was true, Joanne hadn't been blessed with the privileged life that had been advantaged to him.

Luke admired that Joanne had risen above the hand that had been dealt to her to be where she was today. Luke understood that without her will and determination and the strength of her convictions, her life could have followed a very different path. It was apparent that Joanne had challenged herself to do better, and failing had not been an option. Instinctively, Luke sensed that he knew exactly how to fix the issues between them. Joanne was clearly a woman who responded to a challenge, and Luke was intent on giving her one. The light-bulb moment had him grinning from ear to ear.

Mrs. Woodrow, the octogenarian who sat beside him, chuckled into his ear, her voice low as if the two were conspiring together. "Don't know that she ever been married or nothin'. Ain't never seen her wit' no man since I been comin' here."

"Is that right?" Luke whispered back, dealing another hand of gin rummy.

The old woman nodded. "Hear she live in 'dem apartments over on Fourth Street. You know the ones I'm talking 'bout, 'dem go'berment projects just befo' you gets to the schoolhouse."

"Yes, ma'am, I know those."

"Now, 'um not one to gossip, but I hear her mama use to clean houses to put her through 'dat college she went to."

Amusement painted his expression. "You don't say! What about her father? What did he do?"

"Don't know 'dat she had no daddy. But you might want to ask Miss Lucy. She 'da one come every Wednesday for the clinic with 'dat bad wig." The woman shook her head, her expression voicing her displeasure. "Wig all tore up! And it's so red! A woman her age don't need to be wearing no red hair!"

Luke laughed. "Maybe you should give her some tips, Mrs. Woodrow. Everyone knows you have some of the prettiest hair around here."

Devilment shimmered in the old woman's eyes. She giggled softly, waving one frail hand in Luke's direction as she pulled the other through the wealth of silver curls she wore. "Hush yo' mouth!"

Luke gave her a dazzling smile, moving the woman to giggle even more. "Sure looks pretty to me, Mrs. Woodrow," he said, flattering her shamelessly.

"Gin!" the woman cackled, snapping her cards to the table.

The man shook his head. "Young lady, you keep distracting me! I'm never going to win a hand if you keep this up." He smiled brightly.

Mrs. Woodrow grinned, thin lips pulling back over ill-fitting dentures. She leaned in close, her voice dropping an octave as she resumed her whispering. "A girl like Joanne just needs to find her a good man. She spends too much time down here at this center. All the mens here are either old, married, worthless or all the above." The woman tapped Luke's chest with a wrinkled finger. "Yup, Joanne needs her a good man. You don't have you a wife, do you?"

A smile pulled at Luke's mouth. "No, ma'am, I don't."

"Didn't think so. 'Cause if you did you wouldn't a had no biz'ness to be asking so many questions about Joanne."

The conversation was interrupted as little Bryson eased his way between them, leaning a bony elbow on Mrs. Woodrow's knee. The woman chuckled softly as she brushed a hand over his head, patting the child gently against his back. "What 'chu want, baby?"

"Mizz Joanne wants Mr. Luke. She wants some help wit' some boxes."

"What 'da magic word?" the old woman scolded gently.

"P'ease. She said p'ease come help wit' da boxes, Mr. Luke."

"I sure will. Thank you, Bryson," Luke said, moving onto his feet. "Would you like to take my place and play cards with Mrs. Woodrow?"

The young boy grinned widely. "Can we play Go Fish? I like 'dat game."

Mrs. Woodrow skewed her face, her cheeks sinking as if she'd bitten into something sour. "I don't think I knows 'dat game, baby."

"I'll show you, okay?" Bryson said, reaching for the deck of cards. "I'll show you good!"

Leaving the two to maneuver through Bryson's version of Go Fish, Luke sauntered over to where Joanne was waiting. A hopeful expression blessed the woman's face, her usual reserve heightened with a touch of anxiety. She met his smile with a faint one of her own.

"I didn't mean to interrupt, but one of the local restaurants just donated cases of canned goods for the food bank and we need as many hands as we can to get them off the truck."

"No problem. I'm glad to be of service," Luke answered,

following behind as she led the way to the delivery bay at the rear of the building. "So, how are you doing today?"

Joanne nodded. "I'm well, thank you," she responded. She cringed, painfully aware that her formal responses and extended periods of silence were starting to wear thin. She was grateful that he was behind her, unable to see the dismay on her face.

The man had been volunteering for well over a week, and when she hadn't been avoiding him, she would only allow them to exchange fragments of polite conversation until she could find reason to turn tail and run. She could only imagine what he had to be thinking about her. But this wasn't her, and Joanne didn't have a clue why she was reacting so nervously to Luke being around. But his presence was working her nerves like no other man had ever done before.

Joanne couldn't begin to explain why Luke Stallion had her so anxious, but every time she was near him she broke out into a cold sweat. The first few times they'd encountered each other it had been Luke who'd been bumbling and stumbling with anxiety. Now suddenly he was too cool, too smooth and too cocky as he strutted around the center like a prize bull. Joanne, on the other hand, couldn't seem to get it together.

Luke continued to chat as if nothing was awkward between them. He suddenly paused, stopping in his tracks as he gently touched her shoulder, moving Joanne to stop in hers.

Luke took a step forward, sandwiching Joanne between him and the wall. He resisted the urge to draw his finger along the curve of her cheek, wanting to relish the sensation of her silken skin.

"I just wanted you to know that I wasn't offended by your attitude the other day."

"Excuse me?" Startled, Joanne lifted her eyes to stare at him, her eyebrows raised as high as the pitch in her voice.

He repeated himself. "That attitude you gave me. In case you were concerned, I didn't take it personally." The look on Luke's face was smug, amusement gleaming in his eyes. His gaze was so deep that Joanne felt every nerve ending in her body stiffen.

Clearly peeved by his assertion, she suddenly crossed her arms over her chest, one foot tapping the concrete floor anxiously. She forced herself to bite back a caustic reply, saying instead, "I don't recall giving you *attitude*. I was just expressing an opinion." She was a bit chagrined by his arrogance, but that stare was unnerving her more. She found herself fighting not to stare back. She made herself focus on the fire alarm box that decorated the wall right behind his head.

"Clearly you misinterpreted our conversation. I was just expressing my point," she said, hoping that there was much attitude in her reply.

Luke chuckled. "Oh, really. Well, I appreciate that. As you can see, I took your opinion to heart. That's why I'm volunteering."

Joanne drew a hand beneath her chin, her fingers falling against her neck. "Good for you."

"I thought you'd be happy about that."

"You have to do what works for you, Mr. Stallion, not what works for me."

Luke nodded slowly. "What would work for me is if you and I could start all over again. Somehow I think we got off on the wrong foot, and I'd like to make up for that. I hope we can be friends. I would really like for us to be good friends." Luke took a step toward her, seeming to tower above her full frame. "Maybe we can do dinner tonight? If you're not busy?"

Unnerved, Joanne took a step back, moving right up against the egg-shell-colored wall, visibly shaken by the nearness of him. The smile that pulled at his full lips seemed to widen with understanding. Luke sensed that he'd touched a nerve.

What audacity! Joanne mused as she slipped to her left side, needing to put some space between the two of them. She spun about on her heels, feeling as if she were about to break out into a full gallop. As the man sauntered easily behind her, she still didn't bother to answer his question.

Minutes later, with their chore accomplished, Luke brushed the dust from his hands onto his jeans. His gaze met Joanne's again, the woman fighting not to stare at him. He sensed that she wanted to say something, the words seemingly caught on her tongue. He didn't give her an opportunity, instead saying what he had hoped to say before.

"Do you dance, Joanne?"

"Excuse me?"

"Dance. Do you dance?" he repeated.

Joanne leaned her weight on one full hip. She met his stare. "I can."

"Do you salsa?"

Joanne smiled. "I do."

"There's a great club in downtown Dallas called the Tom Cat Club. Do you know it?"

Recognition painted her expression. "I've heard of it," she said casually.

"It's a nice place. The food is good and the music is on point. A group of us get together every now and then for dinner and dancing. I was thinking that maybe you could join us tonight. It's a group thing. Are you interested?"

A pregnant pause filled the space between them as Joanne assessed her options. *If I say yes, then he might think I'm interested in him. If I say no, then he might think I'm not interested in him. But it isn't a date. It's a group thing. A group date couldn't be taken the wrong way. I could do a group thing.* Joanne blew a deep sigh, second thoughts flooding her mind. It wasn't a good idea for her to be mixing center business with personal pleasure. But then again, she hadn't gone out in ages. And dinner and dancing might be fun. After all, it wasn't like they would be alone together, and he needed to know that Joanne Lake didn't have attitude!

"That sounds like fun," she finally answered, her cheeks heated. She inhaled, filling her lungs with air, then blowing it past her pink-tinted lips. "I'd love to."

Luke grinned broadly. "Great. I'll meet you there around seven o'clock."

She nodded. "I'll see you then."

"See you later, buddy!" he chimed as he lifted his hand in a quick good-bye and moved down the hall away from her.

Watching until he disappeared out of sight, Joanne shook her head in dismay. *Buddy?*

Chapter 7

Joanne was throwing clothes around her bedroom when her doorbell sounded. The ring was unexpected, startling her from her thoughts as she debated slacks or a skirt for her evening with Luke Stallion. She wasn't expecting company, and she knew it wasn't her friend Marley, who was supposed to be en route from her job at Starbucks to her philosophy class at the university.

Moving to the door, Joanne peered through the peephole, her expression shifting from curious to annoyed. She had half a mind to ignore the man standing on the other side of the wooden door, but then he rang the bell again, this time holding it longer than necessary, seeming to demand a response from her.

Joanne opened the door reluctantly, annoyance greeting annoyance, as she and her father locked gazes. It had been over a month since he'd last bothered to grace her doorstep.

"What took you so long?" Dr. Charles Lake questioned, leaning to kiss his daughter's cheek as he pushed his way into her home.

"Hi, Daddy," Joanne responded, not bothering to answer his question as she closed the door behind him.

Dr. Lake smiled, nodding his head. "I would have called first, but I was on my way to meet the mayor for dinner and had a few minutes to kill, so I thought I'd drop these papers off to you," he said, waving a large manila envelope at her. "How are you?"

Joanne nodded. "I'm fine. How are you?"

"I've been busy. Extremely busy. There's a lot going on at the office."

His daughter shrugged. "There always is. Would you like something to drink?"

He shook his head. "No. I just stopped to say hello. How's business?"

His question took Joanne by surprise, her father rarely asking about or supporting her design venture. Her excitement seeped into her voice. "It's going very well. I've taken on two new stores and expanded the studio space. I would love for you to stop by and check it out," Joanne said expectantly.

Looking everything but enthusiastic, Dr. Lake nodded. "Sure. So are you still spending all your time downtown at that center?"

Joanne paused briefly before answering. "I'm still volunteering."

"Just like your mother," he mumbled under his breath, as if there were something wrong with Joanne having any similarities to the woman who'd given birth to her.

Joanne heaved a deep sigh, warm breath blowing into the cool air. "I was actually on my way out, as well. Maybe we can get together for lunch later this week?" Her expression was hopeful. Her father's response was less than eager.

"Maybe. I'll have to check my schedule." Dr. Lake gestured with the envelope he was still holding. "You need to put these away somewhere safe. I've added some stocks to your portfolio. One day you need to sit down with myself or my accountant and go over them so you understand what you have."

Crossing her arms over her chest, Joanne stared at the envelope before moving her gaze to her father's face. "Yes, Daddy," she said, enthusiasm waning from her tone. "Thank you, but I really don't think you should keep—"

Her father interrupted her, tossing the envelope onto the table in the center of the room. "Don't argue. These investments are for your future, Joanne. If you won't invest in it, I certainly will." He looked around her home one last time. "I really don't know why you insist on living here on your own like this when we have that big house."

"That's your house."

"No, Joanne, it's our home. You left because you wanted to, not because you had to. You can come home whenever you want."

Joanne sighed again, not interested in waging another argument about the same topics the two constantly butted heads over. She appeased him instead. "Yes, sir. I know."

The man nodded, his gaze shifting toward her as he looked her up and down. "Are you eating properly, Joanne? I really hope you're not gorging on junk food. You really need to try to get some of that weight off. It's not healthy for you."

Joanne bristled, her expression voicing her irritation. "Thanks for the tip, Daddy. I'll get right on that."

Completely oblivious, her father smiled, taking a step

toward her. He placed his hands on her shoulders, pulling her to him as he wrapped her in a warm hug.

"Take care of yourself, Joanne."

Her eyes closed, Joanne pressed her face into her father's chest. "I love you, Daddy."

Kissing her forehead, Dr. Lake moved back to the door. "I'll call you soon. Okay?"

Nodding, Joanne sauntered behind him. "Goodbye, Daddy."

Even before she could close the door behind him, tears had misted behind Joanne's eyelids. She wiped at the moisture with the heel of her hand. She refused to cry, adamant that she would not shed one single tear over her father. She'd been wasting tears on the man for too many years.

Reaching for the envelope he'd dropped onto her coffee table, Joanne didn't bother to look inside, hardly interested in the newly purchased stock she knew to be detailed inside. Joanne had little interest in the many investments her father had made on her behalf, the man believing that such would afford Joanne the only security she would ever need. Moving into the kitchen, she pulled open the silverware drawer and dropped the mailer inside, along with the other forty or so unopened envelopes hidden behind her few spoons and forks.

Dr. Charles Lake had been trying to buy her affections since she'd been six years old when he had won sole custody of her from her actress mother. Lillian Taylor, beaten and broken from the nasty legal battle he'd waged, had crossed an ocean to put as much space between her and him as she could. Leaving had garnered her more alone time with her only child than staying for a few hours of weekly visitation ever would have. The doctor had tried to buy that away from them, too, but his money hadn't been able to get him everything he'd wanted.

Joanne's father was a man who assessed his entire life by his material wealth. He didn't consider himself accomplished if he wasn't making money and more money. He'd come from money, his parents affording him the best of everything with their oil ventures. His father had insisted he go to medical school. As a little girl, Joanne remembered him having a thriving surgical practice. Business had kept him away more than it had kept him home. When she'd complained, there had always been a new toy to appease her.

Joanne had wanted for very little. What she'd been desperate for was time and attention, the two things her father never seemed to have for her. The day Joanne had turned eighteen, she'd made the decision to live her life very differently from her father's life. Attending design school on the West Coast had afforded her much anonymity. Returning to Dallas, but far from her father, had kept her under the radar.

Very few of her own friends and associates knew anything about her, and Joanne was determined to keep it that way. She'd had a pampered and privileged upbringing, and now she wanted her life to be more about helping those who were much less fortunate.

A few years ago the good Dr. Lake had laid down his scalpel, giving up medicine altogether. Building upon his own father's initial investments had become his new goal of choice. Bonding with his daughter hadn't yet made his list of things to do.

Even at the age of six, Joanne had understood that her mother staying would have left them both damaged beyond repair. Her father's bitterness toward his ex-wife was palpable. The man had thrived on his resentment. He and his money would have made their lives a living hell, so instead, Joanne frequently flew to Paris to spend time with her mom. The two women eventually built a thriving relationship that her father hadn't been able to tarnish with the money he tossed around like water.

Thinking of her mother, Joanne suddenly had the urge to hear her voice and to ask her advice about men, one man in particular. Taking a quick glance at the grandfather clock on the far wall she realized that with the time difference, a call would be wasted since Lillian would be in the theater, readying herself to perform the lead role in the stage production of *Carmen*. Joanne decided she would call her mother later. Just maybe, she thought, she might be able to maneuver her schedule and fly to France for an extended weekend. Mother's Day was just around the corner, and it would make for a nice surprise.

Returning to her bedroom, she reached for the new chocolate-brown skirt she'd purchased from Ashley Stewart, the skirt having won the debate with her tailored black slacks. The top would be one of her own designs, a form fitting V-neck shirt in a bold, animal print. Brown suede ankle boots would complete the look. Minutes later, pressed, pampered and perfumed, Joanne headed out the door, excited and anxious to see Luke Stallion again.

When Joanne arrived at the Tom Cat Club, parking her car a good distance from the front entrance, her nerves were a tangled mess. She took a deep breath, filling her lungs with the warm evening air. Taking one last look at her reflection in the rearview mirror, she dabbed a light coat of tinted lip gloss to her lips.

She didn't have a clue what to expect, not wanting to imagine the *friends* that might be with Luke. She only hoped that none of them recognized her or knew her father.

She wasn't ready for Luke Stallion to know so much about her personal life.

What she did want, though, was to spend more time with Luke, to get to know him better. Joanne was anxious to discover whether there was truly more to him than met the eye. The man excited Joanne, and she'd been fighting it with everything she had in her, but there was no denying the attraction between them. On the surface, Luke Stallion represented what she disliked most about her own father. But clearly there was something to that man that had her intrigued.

There were two bouncers at the door of the Tom Cat Club, both looking like oversized Buddhas busting out of too-small, pin-striped suits. One had a clipboard in his large hand, only allowing admittance as the moment moved him. Joanne assessed the long line of partygoers hoping to be allowed inside. The women were all stylishly underdressed, the men elaborately overdressed. They were a pretty crowd of Dallas's young elite, mixing and mingling like an assortment of sweet confections. She didn't waste any energy with the end of the line, strutting boldly straight to the front door.

Buddha Number One gave her a smug look, eyeing her from head to toe. Joanne knew instantly that she didn't fit the profile of the size 0 beauties in short-short, low-cut attire that typically got in without a hassle. But Joanne was hardly intimidated. She eyed both the Buddhas with disdain.

"May we help you?" Buddha Number Two asked, his soft voice seeming out of place for his massive size.

Joanne smiled sweetly. "I'm meeting Luke Stallion. My name's Joanne."

Buddha Number One chuckled. "You're meeting Mr. Stallion? And we're supposed to believe that?"

Joanne's eyes narrowed to thin slits. "I don't much care what you believe. Check your list."

The man fingered the document clipped to his clipboard, not bothering to even glance down at it. "I don't see a Joanne on the guest list," he said snidely.

Joanne reached into her purse and pulled her state-issued ID and a small photograph of her and her father from her wallet. She passed it to the man. "Look again," she said sternly.

Both men eyed the documents quickly, then passed them back to her.

"Miss Lake, our apology," Buddha Number One said as he reached for the velvet rope that cordoned off the entrance from the general public. "Please, go right on in," the man said, waving her inside.

Before heading through the door, Joanne turned from one to the other, her expression stern. "I really don't like either one of you, but if you two want to keep your jobs, you don't know me, is that clear?" she said, her tone firm.

The Buddha nodded his thick neck. "Yes, ma'am."

"Enjoy your evening," the second man echoed.

Her sweet smiling returning, Joanne brushed past them both. Before the club's front door was closed behind her she heard a potential partygoer complaining about her cutting the line. The response echoed harshly behind her.

"What do you want from me? Ownership has its privileges."

The nightclub was filled to capacity. Pretty people filled tables, the dance floor, the length of the bar and crowded the aisle Joanne walked to enter the main party room. Inside, the décor was minimalistic, simple black tables and black chairs with a black-and-white checked floor. The lighting was dim and seductive, and bright white balloons and vibrant red streamers crowded the ceiling.

They were playing reggae, the music beckoning to her as bass drums vibrated within the concealed speakers in the walls. Iridescent lights flickered above her head, and the smell of sweat mingled with a mélange of perfumes and colognes. Around her, bodies were gyrating and twisting with the music, the couples lost in the beat of their own rhythms.

Even with the crowd, there was no missing Luke Stallion, the man's commanding presence filling the room. Joanne saw him before he saw her as he stood in conversation with two other young, well-dressed men. She stood watching him curiously, appreciating him from afar. The brother was dressed nicely, a silk suit in a pale shade of gray fitting him nicely. He was leaning back on one hip, his hands pushed casually into the pockets of his slacks. He was animated, energy seeping from his pores, and Joanne was suddenly thankful that she'd decided to come.

As she continued watching him, she couldn't miss the too-cute female who sauntered to his side mid-conversation to whisper into his ear. The woman was svelte with a close-cropped bob, a milky complexion and bright eyes begging for attention. Luke nodded his head as he listened to whatever it was she was telling him, a wry smile pulling at his mouth. As if to make her point, the too-cute female pressed a manicured hand to his chest, drawing it slowly down to his abdomen and around his waist. A wave of something that felt like jealousy rippled over Joanne's spirit.

Shaking her head slightly, Joanne contemplated turning around and going back home. Clearly the man had enough friends to keep him company, so he probably wouldn't even notice if she didn't show up. But she couldn't pull herself from where she stood as she continued watching him and the young woman, who was clearly eager for his time. Her mind was almost made up when Luke caught sight of her, his eyes focused straight in her direction. His wry smile pulled into a full grin.

As the two locked gazes, a rush of heat flushed Joanne's face with color. She inhaled deeply to stall the quiver of butterflies that suddenly danced deep in her abdomen. Before she could form a coherent thought, the man had excused himself from the group, extracting himself from the other woman's grip, and was striding eagerly in her direction. Joanne could feel herself grinning back as his wide smile greeted her warmly.

"Hey, you!" Luke yelled over the din of music and loud conversations bouncing off the deep red walls. "I was afraid you weren't going to show up!" He leaned in close to her, pressing his cheek next to hers as he whispered loudly into her ear. His hands rested lightly against her waist, his fingers heating her flesh through her clothes.

Joanne inhaled swiftly. "Why's that?" she answered, forcing herself to take a step back away from his touch. "I told you I would meet you."

Luke shrugged. "I know, but I didn't do a great job of letting you know how badly I wanted you here. I wouldn't have blamed you if you'd changed your mind." Luke reached for her hand, pressing his fingers between hers. "I have a table over there for us."

Leading her past the throng of revelers, Luke guided her across the room to a corner table some distance from the dance floor, the bar and the wealth of noise. It wasn't nearly as loud as the lower level they'd just passed, making it easier for the two of them to hold a conversation.

"So, where are your friends?" Joanne asked as he pulled out a chair for her to sit in.

Luke moved to the other side of the table and sat down. He smiled, a smug expression washing over his face. "I was thinking you're the only friend I wanted to spend time with tonight. I didn't get the impression that you would have come if you thought it would only be you and me here."

Joanne crossed her arms over her chest, eyeing him with some reservation. She hated to admit that he was probably right. She'd been more than ready for some group activity. The very thought of him and her spending time one-on-one would have made her too nervous. Nevertheless, there they were.

Joanne met his gaze, the deep stare shooting heat straight to her southern quadrant. A sly smile pulled at his mouth, and she couldn't stop herself from smiling back. "This amuses you, doesn't it?" she said, chuckling softly.

Luke nodded. "You amuse me. You're a hard woman to read, Joanne Lake, and you've really been giving me a run for my money."

Joanne laughed. "You don't say."

The man nodded. "So, are we friends now?"

She shrugged. "We'll see," she answered, her eyebrows raised ever so slightly. "I'll let you know when the night is over."

Conversation flowed like water. Joanne found herself enjoying the laughter that billowed warmly in the air between them. Luke had taken the liberty of ordering dinner before her arrival, and within minutes of their sitting down, a waiter was serving them a spectacular meal of lobster ravioli with a chocolate soufflé for dessert. Between them they polished off a bottle of very expensive wine, and Joanne found herself falling head over heels into a state of blissful relaxation.

Luke couldn't stop himself from staring at her. Dropping into the dark depths of her gaze, he felt as if he'd found something that had been lost to him since forever. The emotion was startling and comforting at the same time. As they sat in deep discussion, enjoying the meal and the company, he marveled at how easily he was able to open up to her.

Joy spilled out of her eyes as they talked about the center and her business. He marveled at the glow that shone in her face. She spoke passionately about her love for her work and the families she'd come to care for. Time flew as they became acquainted with one another. Luke found himself talking a lot about his life and asking question after question about hers.

"One of the ladies at the center was telling me that you live near the center with your mother. Were you raised in that area?"

Joanne paused, a lie threatening to spill past her lips. She evaded the question instead. "I was raised here and there, nowhere special."

"You don't like talking about yourself, do you?"

"There's not much to talk about." She smiled. "Besides, I'm enjoying talking about you more."

He leaned back in his seat, folding his hands in his lap as he studied her expression. "So, what else can I tell you? What do you want to know about me? I'm an open book, so ask away."

A glint of mischief danced in Joanne's eyes. She leaned forward, her elbows propped on the table as she dropped her chin against the back of her cupped hands.

"How many stamps do you have in your passport?"

"Not enough."

"Have you ever had sex on a first date?"

"No."

"Never?"

Luke smirked. "Never, but I've had sex on a few *last* dates."

Joanne chuckled, shaking her head. "That's so wrong in so many ways."

"Never said I was a Boy Scout. What's the next question?"

Joanne paused for a brief moment. "What's your definition of *foreplay?*"

The man's eyes widened in surprise. He suddenly laughed, mirth rising out of his midsection and flooding his entire body. He laughed hard, the intensity of it moving him to tears. He pressed the cloth napkin in his lap to the corner of his eyes, dabbing at the moisture that had clouded his vision. "That was a good one!"

Joanne laughed with him. "I know. So answer the question."

Luke nodded. "Wow! My definition of *foreplay*," he repeated, enthralled by the energy that spun from her eyes. Pausing, Joanne could see his mind racing for an answer. "Why don't I just show you," he said finally, lifting himself from his seat and extending his hand in her direction.

Joanne was clearly curious as Luke entwined his fingers between hers and pulled her to her feet. She couldn't help but follow behind him as he led her back to the front of the nightclub and the dance floor, which was jam-packed with couples shimmying hot against each other.

The music had a rich Caribbean flavor, calypso beats with a hard bass line. One couldn't help but be moved by the pulsating tones. Pushing his way to the center of the crowd and a small area of empty floor space, Luke turned to face her, his shoulders starting to bounce in time with the music. He raised his arms to chest level, his large hands clasped into tight fists, his torso waving from side to side. Taking a step toward her, his pelvis gyrated seductively, his hips swaying for attention. His eyes were locked on hers, and Joanne could feel herself falling fast into the stare he was giving her.

Joanne began to gyrate her own hips. She danced slowly at first, her body moving instinctively with his. Moving with him was intoxicating. Heat was rising quickly between them, and Joanne suddenly wanted to strip right out of her clothes in exchange for a rush of cool air. When Luke took another step closer, his pelvis meeting hers as his hands fell to her waist, pulling her to him, Joanne thought she could easily pass out from the sudden rush of emotion that flooded through her.

The man was moving against her, his gyrations tight and precise. Joanne couldn't remember when her arms had swept up and around his shoulders until she became aware of her fingers lightly caressing the nape of his neck. Their bodies were pressed so tightly together it was as if they were one unit instead of two. Then Luke pulled some fancy footwork on her, spinning her around so that her back was against his chest as he pushed himself against her buttocks. Unable to resist, Joanne gyrated with him, savoring the sensation of his rock-hard frame kissing the cushion of her soft curves. She raised her arms over her head, her fingers snapping in time to the music. Dancing against him like a stripper on a mission, she lowered herself to floor level and slithered back again, her body never losing contact with his.

Luke slipped his arms back around her waist, spinning her around to face him. The look in his eyes was pure, unadulterated lust, his hunger setting every nerve ending in her body on fire. Both of them felt like they were going to combust, heat radiating from every open pore. As Luke continued to move against her, his left arm holding her tightly around the waist, his right hand moved up the length of her back and his palm came to rest against the back of her head. Then without warning, Luke slipped his fingers into the short length of her hair, his palm cupping the nape of her neck. He tugged gently as he dipped her over his arm.

The gesture took her by surprise, causing Joanne to gasp loudly, and then he leaned down over her, pressing his mouth against the curve of her neck. The sensation of his lips against her bare skin was electrifying, overwhelming her senses, and Joanne moaned loudly, forgetting that they were surrounded by a crowd of people. Desire raged rampant between them. The sensations were intense and unyielding.

Luke planted a soft trail of kisses up the length of her neck toward her chin. Joanne tried to murmur an objection, but only a low hum bubbled past her lips. Her eyes locked with his, and before she could draw her next breath, Luke slowly caressed her mouth with his own, grazing her lips once, and then again, the soft touch teasing.

Joanne pressed her palms to his chest. Her clarity was suddenly skewed, desire sweeping every coherent thought from her. She could barely remember her own name as he lifted her back up. Luke smiled, moving to wrap both arms around her as he pressed his cheek to hers.

He whispered into her ear, his breath blowing hot against her flesh. "I'd say that was just my intro to foreplay. To give you a full definition, I would need a whole weekend alone with you."

Joanne struggled to breathe, words caught tight in her chest as she tried to ignore the hands that glided like hot coals against her skin. The music had transitioned to a slow and seductive tune. Without missing a beat, the two had slowed their roll, their gyrations measured as they continued to move one against the other. A slow smile pulled at her lips as she lifted her eyes back to his.

"I think I get the picture," she said softly, stammering ever so slightly.

Luke smiled back, his expression smug. "Are you sure? Because I don't mind painting a complete portrait for you. I don't mind at all!"

Pushing herself away from him, Joanne glanced quickly around the room. "I'm sure," she said, her gaze returning to his. "I'll have to pass."

Luke eyed her curiously. "Why?"

"Because we're friends. And I don't engage in foreplay with my friends."

Chapter 8

It had been a good night. Luke was still riding high from his time with Joanne. She had allowed him another dance as the music changed and the tempo shifted to something a little faster. Sometime later, both perspiring lightly under the warm lights, he'd pulled her to him tightly, whispered into her ear and guided her back to her seat.

Settling herself back in the cushioned seat, she'd waited patiently while he ran to the men's room, returning to her side as quickly as he could manage. A waiter had appeared with two glasses of merlot, depositing them carefully onto the table. Nodding, Luke had flashed her a toothy smile, winking all-knowingly as though they shared some deep, dark secret.

"Thank you," he'd said loudly over the music, his smile warm and alluring. "You dance beautifully."

Joanne had smiled sweetly in response. "No, thank *you*,"

she'd said warmly. "Twelve years of dance lessons finally paid off."

He'd chuckled, nodding. They'd talked for a while longer and then she'd left, wishing him a good night as she departed. It would have been a very good night if he had been able to convince her to stay, but she wasn't hearing his arguments.

"I would really like to," Joanne had said. "But I'm going to be out of town for a few days. I need to get home and pack. My ride is coming early in the morning."

"Oh? Where are you off to?" Luke had asked, curiosity pulling at him.

Joanne had smiled sweetly, her mouth curving easily toward the ceiling. "I thought I would surprise my mother for Mother's Day."

Luke had nodded his head. "That should be fun. I'm sure she'll love getting out of town for a few days."

Joanne had simply smiled, not bothering to respond or correct him before wishing him a good night. As she had made her exit he had been left staring anxiously after her.

Luke sighed, and then he took in a deep breath of air, filling his lungs. He really liked that woman. It felt good to be in her company. It had felt great to hold her close in his arms. Joanne amused him. She said more with a simple tilt of her head than some women were able to say in hours of conversation. Staring into her eyes he'd thought of a chocolate pool, the warm orbs cool and calculating.

Noting every detail of each other, the evening had gone better than expected. Luke knew she had been feeling him, as well. He was sure of it. His face bloomed into a wide grin. He was certain Joanne Lake was feeling something for him, too, and he knew one way to be sure.

Pulling his car off the main roadway, he came to a stop,

shifted the transmission into park and reached for his cell phone. He dialed the last number in his call list, anxious for the party to answer on the other end. When she did, Luke fought to contain his excitement.

"Joanne, hey! I hope I didn't catch you at a bad time."

The young woman chuckled softly. "Not at all. Is something the matter?"

"No, why would you ask that?"

"Maybe, because I just left you? I thought we just said goodbye for the night."

"We did, but I had a brilliant idea," he said, wincing. He was suddenly thankful that she couldn't see the embarrassment that crossed his face. He could only imagine what she must have been thinking. Maybe his good idea hadn't been that good after all.

"And what was that?" Joanne asked curiously.

"Lemon meringue pie!" His excitement registered over the phone line.

Joanne laughed again. "Would you care to elaborate?"

"There's a great little place I know that serves the best lemon meringue pie in the whole world. I'm dying to share a piece with you, and I figured it's still early, so why not? You game?" He paused, anxious for her reaction.

"You mean right now?"

"Yes. Now is as good a time as any."

Joanne was suddenly intrigued. She stammered, trying to think of one good reason why she shouldn't. "I have to... pack...and...tomorrow, we—"

"It's not even ten o'clock yet and it's only pie. One slice. Besides, I'm not ready to end our evening. I would really love to spend just a little while longer with you. What do you say?"

Joanne smiled into the receiver, touched by the hopefulness in his tone. "I guess one slice can't hurt me."

Ten minutes later Joanne pulled her car into the empty parking space beside his. By the time she had shut off her engine and unbuckled her seat belt, Luke was standing at her door, his hand on the latch, ready to open it. Joanne took a deep breath before stepping out of the vehicle.

When Luke leaned forward, gently kissing her cheek, she hadn't been at all prepared for the affectionate greeting. Her knees began to shake uncontrollably, her legs threatening to drop her back down to her seat. Before she realized it, he'd taken her hand in his own, clutching it tightly as he entwined his fingers with hers.

"I'm glad you came," he said, his voice dropping to a low whisper.

Joanne smiled sweetly. "Lemon meringue is my favorite." She looked over her shoulder toward the entrance to the twenty-four-hour diner. "So this is the place that serves the best pie in the world?"

Luke laughed, shaking his head. "No. This was just a convenient place for us to meet." He opened the passenger door of his car, gesturing for her to take a seat. "Let's ride!"

As Luke guided her to the waiting helicopter, Joanne's eyes widened, reluctance dropping like a blanket around her. She couldn't begin to fathom how or why the two of them were standing in wait on the heliport atop the Stallion corporate office in search of some lemon meringue pie.

The copter's pilot greeted them both cheerfully, as if flying folks around in the middle of the night was something he did every day. Both men ignored Joanne's feeble protests as Luke helped her into the aircraft, strapping her securely in her seat.

"This is ridiculous," she sputtered, glancing from side to side.

Luke chuckled warmly. "Maybe, but since we can, why not?"

She rolled her eyes skyward. "Where are we going?"

"We're going to shoot down to Houston. That's where my favorite little café is."

"In Houston?"

He nodded. "Yep, and the best coffee, too!"

Secured in his own seat, Luke dropped a casual hand against her knee, his palm caressing her gently. He seemed to sense her misgivings as he leaned in to whisper into her ear.

"You don't look relaxed. Is everything okay?"

Joanne closed her eyes briefly, taking a deep inhale of breath. She couldn't begin to tell him that nothing was okay, as a wealth of emotion exploded within her. Her mind and her body were suddenly battling for control. She wasn't supposed to be feeling the swell of sensations sweeping through her, desire rising like a rampant fire. Instead, she just nodded, lifting her gaze to meet his. "I'm fine, thank you," she muttered before turning to stare out to the darkened sky.

The city of Dallas swelled full and large beneath them, lights shimmering against the nocturnal landscape. Staring below, Joanne could just make out the Fairmont Hotel, the Dallas Museum of Art, Lincoln Plaza and the Trammel Crowe Center before the city disappeared from sight. As the helicopter moved swiftly toward its destination, the trip was feeling quite surreal to her.

Luke moved his hand from her knee, draping his arm along the back of her shoulders. The gentle glide of his fingertips over the length of her arm wasn't helping the situation. His touch was like lighter fluid the way heat exploded from the center of her feminine spirit. Joanne resisted the urge to let herself settle comfortably against him, the desire to be cradled against his side consuming. She desperately wished she could move, to put a hint of distance between them, but there was nowhere for her to go.

The 240-mile trip from Dallas to Houston lasted just under an hour before the helicopter was touching down on the helipad. Joanne didn't need to ask where they were, as the Stallion logo loomed high above the building on the roof. She heaved a deep sigh. Something in the back of her mind was whispering that she should have told the man no.

The owner of the Little Moccasin Café was a spirited soul with a bald dome the color of honeyed nuts. The old man greeted them both warmly, tapping a heavy hand against Luke's back.

"Good to see you again, kid! It's been a while. And who might this pretty little thing be?"

"It's good to see you, too, Mr. Jessup. This is my friend Joanne," he said, introducing the two. "You're not closing up already, are you? We came a long way for some of your wife's pie."

Mr. Jessup grinned a toothless grin. "Nah! You know we open all night long, kid." He led them to a side booth, gesturing for them to take a seat. "Your usual?" he asked, not bothering to wait for a response as he headed back toward the kitchen.

Luke laughed softly. "Thank you, Mr. Jessup," he called after the old guy.

Joanne tilted her head. "How often do you get down here?" she asked, her curiosity heightened.

Luke shrugged. "Every now and again."

"You just saddle up your helicopter and jet on down when the moment moves you, huh?"

Luke smiled, his eyes widening as he noted the cynicism rising in her tone. "Something like that."

She shook her head. The man was unbelievably spoiled, she thought. She couldn't believe how nonchalant he was about having flown miles just to get a slice of dessert. Then she tasted the pie.

The two slices of savory lemon confection the restaurant's owner sat down on the table before them were heavenly. The sweet dessert sat in a puddle of warm, dark chocolate with a dollop of fresh whipped cream adorning the picture-perfect meringue.

Luke's gaze was locked on her face as Joanne took her first bite, savoring the decadent flavors slowly. The smile that suddenly pulled at her mouth, lifting her lips, dazzled him. "I told you it was the best," he chimed excitedly.

Joanne stifled a laugh, pulling a yellow paper napkin to her mouth as she swallowed. "Yes, you did," she said as she pulled a second bite to her lips. "And you were right. It's very good."

"Worth the trip?"

Joanne lifted her eyes to stare into his. The look he gave her shimmered with excitement. Joanne was mesmerized by the energy that seemed to detonate her own. She nodded her head slowly, joy washing over her expression as she answered. "Very."

When Joanne crawled beneath the sheets of her bed, turning off the light on the nightstand by the bedside, it was almost three o'clock in the morning. She was still trying to absorb the events of the evening—everything about her time with Luke Stallion was like nothing she'd ever experienced on any date before. Drunk with joy, Joanne's excitement still bubbled like water from a fresh spring. With the way she was feeling, she fathomed that she'd never be able to fall asleep before her alarm announced that it was time for her to rise and shine.

Joanne couldn't remember the last time she'd had so much fun. Their conversation had continued without skipping a beat as they'd enjoyed their pie and coffee. The man had made her laugh, eventually acknowledging his reluctance to even ask her to join him on their excursion. Joanne couldn't help but admit that despite her initial reluctance she'd been thrilled that he had.

She also couldn't help but admit that she was feeling guilty about them having shared such an extravagant evening when so many of the clients she served couldn't begin to fathom such an opportunity. Luke hadn't helped her with her conflict, the man having not an ounce of regret for his actions.

"I wanted to spend time with you," he'd said, leaning back against the cushioned booth seat. "Why does my wanting to show you a good time have to be a crime?"

"It isn't," Joanne had answered, his admission moving her to lift her eyes in wonder. "It's just—"

"Joanne, I don't often meet a woman who I want to share moments like this with. You're an incredibly beautiful woman, inside and out. I have the resources to show you a spectacular time, and I want to do just that. I want to share the things I enjoy most with you. Let me. Please?"

The man's smile had been as sweet as a gentle rain on a sun-kissed afternoon. He'd leaned forward in his seat, reaching for both her hands as he'd clasped her fingers beneath his large palms. His look had been beseeching, his glazed eyes peering deep into hers. Joanne had fallen headfirst into his dark stare, completely enamored with Luke and the moment. With her resistance weakened, she hadn't been able to find the words to give him a counter argument.

Rolling to the other side of the bed, Joanne heaved a deep sigh. As she drifted off into the warmth of a good night's sleep, Luke Stallion filled her thoughts, nicely flooding her dreams.

Joanne was still thinking about Luke as she made the cross continental flight to Paris, France. She was grateful for the reprieve, a few days of down time to reflect on what she was feeling and get some perspective from an unbiased party. She smiled, knowing her mother would surely have an opinion about Joanne and her relationship with *any* man. She also knew it would hardly be impartial.

Joanne hadn't given it much thought before, but she was grateful that she and her mother had a relationship at all. No thanks to her father, the two women had been able to form an extraordinary bond with one another. Joanne was acutely aware that not everyone was as fortunate.

Luke had told her he had no memories of his own mother. The woman had died when he'd been very young. During one of their many conversations he'd admitted to feeling like he'd missed out on something very special.

Joanne turned to stare out the airplane's window, her eyes skating across the ice blue sky. Luke had mentioned on more than one occasion how much he looked forward to meeting Joanne's parents. And Joanne had promised to make those introductions. She just hadn't assured her new friend that it would be any time soon.

As the pilot turned on the seatbelt sign, announcing their descent, Joanne shook her head. She had much to tell her mother. She trusted that her mother would have a wealth of advice to give back to her.

Lillian Taylor was standing in wait in the terminal of

the Charles de Gaulle International airport. A wide grin spread across Joanne's face the moment she saw the woman smiling warmly and waving her arms excitedly in Joanne's direction.

"Mommy!" Joanne exclaimed as she rushed into her mother's arms, yielding to the emotion that pulled at her heartstrings. Salty tears dampened her eyes as her mother held her tightly.

Lillian Taylor drew her hands across her daughter's back and shoulders, caressing her gently. *"Bonjour, le bébé.* How is my darling daughter?"

"I'm glad to see you," Joanne exclaimed, her eyes meeting her mother's intense gaze. And she was, marveling at how little her mother had changed since her last visit.

Lillian's rich black hair was pulled back into a loose chignon atop her head, wisps of tendrils framing her face. Her complexion was flawless, her makeup regime only including a hint of lipstick, dark eyeliner to accent her wide eyes and a faint layer of mascara painting her eyelashes. She hugged her mother a second time.

Lillian nodded, hugging the young woman back. "So what has your father done now, *chérie*?" she asked, maternal intuition kicking in.

Joanne shook her head. "Daddy hasn't done anything. I just missed you is all, and I have so much I want to tell you."

"Well, I have missed you too, *chérie*. But I can tell there is something more going on with you. What is it?"

Joanne smiled, color rising to her full cheeks. "I've met someone. A really great guy, Mommy!"

Her mother smiled back. "Oh, *chérie*! I can't wait to hear all about him."

As the two women looped their arms and headed toward

the baggage claim area, Joanne leaned her head on her mother's shoulder.

"Happy Mother's Day," she said softly. "Happy Mother's Day!"

Chapter 9

It had been one very long week since their excursion for pie. Luke had been anxious to see Joanne again, impatient for her to return from her extended trip with her mother. Anticipating her return he'd left her a voice mail message, and then two, hopeful that she would give him a call.

When that return call finally came, Joanne was inviting him to join her at a neighborhood tenants' meeting. Her clients had been displaced by the landlord's failure to maintain his property to city code and needed support. Luke had been more than ready and willing to join her.

Joanne had greeted him warmly, her own excitement spreading like wildfire across her face. "Luke, hello, it's good to see you again."

Luke smiled brightly. "I'm glad you called, Joanne." He leaned to kiss her cheek. "I missed you," he said, his voice dropping to a husky whisper.

Joanne blushed profusely, having no response as she ushered him into city hall.

Inside the large conference room the atmosphere was tense, tenants fueling the air with fear and anger. With their apartment building condemned, families had suddenly found themselves rudely evicted with nowhere to go. The community center had stepped in to find them housing and represent their interests.

The meeting had been emotionally challenging, and afterward tension painted Joanne's face, her whole body shaking from the experience. Sensing that she needed a few minutes to vent and unwind, Luke suggested they take a short walk, hoping it would help to alleviate some of her stress.

Side by side they maneuvered their way through the rose gardens of the Historical Park, the public haven blooming full and bright with summer flora. The air was scented with the light fragrance of freesia and roses, and above their heads the blue sky had been bright and clear.

"Do you go to many of these meetings?" Luke asked, his eyes flitting easily across her face.

"Too many of them," Joanne muttered, wrapping her arms around her shoulders. She met his gaze, a slight smile pulling at her mouth. "But when we can accomplish something that benefits our clients, I know there isn't anything else I'd rather be doing."

Luke nodded his head. "So, tell me about your design business."

A wide smile filled Joanne's face, the energy gleaming in her eyes. "Now, that's my passion. I love creating wearable art for women who look like me."

"I can see where clothing beautiful women could be appealing."

Joanne chuckled softly. "Most especially women of size."

Luke's eyebrows rose with amusement. "We men love us a well-dressed woman with luscious curves now!"

"I just bet you do," Joanne laughed warmly.

Laughing with her, Luke snaked his hand over hers, clasping her fingers between his own. Swinging their arms between them, he tossed her a wide grin. The smile Joanne gave him back took his breath away.

Hand in hand they continued to chat easily, Joanne sharing her experiences with navigating a new business as Luke listened intently. Walking her back to her car, he was less than thrilled to see their afternoon end. The more he learned about the delightful woman, the more he wanted to know. He was discovering just how truly special Joanne Lake was.

The next day Luke rose early, the morning air teasing his senses. His sleep had been unsettling, Joanne Lake haunting his dreams. Luke had never before felt for any woman what he found himself feeling for Joanne. The woman excited him, making him feel like a giddy teenager. Joanne had a way of reaching deep into his spirit and pulling the best from him. He loved that when he was with her he wanted to be a better man.

As he made his way across town, he couldn't shake the memories of their time together from his mind. Pulling his car around the circular driveway of Briscoe Ranch he heaved a deep sigh, thankful for a distraction.

Luke couldn't miss the wealth of activity spinning around the ranch as the site was being prepared for the annual Black Rodeo event they were hosting. The ranch had become a second home to him and his brothers when John and Marah had merged their two families. Luke couldn't begin to imagine his life without them, or the homestead.

Stepping out of his parked car, he turned to stare out at the landscape.

Briscoe Ranch was some eight hundred acres of working cattle ranch and an equestrian center. It also housed an entertainment complex that specialized in corporate and private client services with two 20,000 square-foot event barns and a country bed-and-breakfast. Central to Austin, Houston, Dallas and Fort Worth, Briscoe Ranch had made quite a name for itself.

Last year John and his wife had acquired controlling interest in the property under the Stallion umbrella and it had become his brother Matthew's pet project. Newly instilled community outreach programs and a mentoring program for at-risk youth had broadened the scope of how they did business. John frequently said that as their investments went, Briscoe Ranch was clearly the best decision they had ever made. Not one of the Stallion brothers would disagree.

Edward and Juanita Briscoe both greeted him at the door, Edward pulling the structure open as Luke stepped onto the porch.

"Well, good morning there, young fella'," the man chimed. "How are you this morning?"

Luke grinned. "Just fine, sir. How about yourself?"

The man's head bobbed up and down. "This woman is about to drive me crazy, but I'm surviving!"

"Good morning, Aunt Juanita!"

Juanita rolled her eyes. "Luke, baby, don't pay this fool no never mind." She leaned up to kiss his cheek. "Breakfast is just about ready. Go on in. Everyone's in the back."

Nodding, Luke made his way into the home, shaking his head as the duo fussed at each other about a tent that wasn't being placed where Juanita thought it should be. He smiled warmly as he turned to stare back at the couple.

Juanita had helped raise him. The woman had been his parents' best friend, stepping in to give John a hand when their mother and father had been killed in the automobile accident. Luke had only been eight years old. Just weeks before John and Marah's wedding, her father, Edward, had married Juanita, further merging the two families into one. Luke was the first to admit that he loved how their little family had grown.

Continuing down the hallway, familiar banter greeted him at the entrance to the large kitchen and the family room at the rear of the home. His brothers were already there, the trio sitting at attention as they waited for the morning meal.

Marah and her twin sister, Marla, were flipping pancakes on the stovetop, the two women engaged in debate over a recent bill passed by the Dallas board of education. Marah's older sister, Eden, and her husband were reviewing the proof for that weekend's program, anxious to get it to the printer right after the meal. The rest of the family was chatting and laughing, enjoying their weekly ritual of camaraderie and fellowship.

Entering the space, Luke called out a warm greeting. As if they'd practiced it to perfection, the group greeted him in unison like a backup band in perfect sync. "Luke!"

He leaned to kiss Marah and Marla's cheeks and then moved to hug Michelle and Eden. Slipping into the seat between John and Marla's husband, Mike, the men gave each other a fist-bump hello.

"How's it going?" John asked, reaching for a large glass of orange juice.

Luke shrugged. "I'm making progress."

John sipped his drink. "Progress is good. Any problems?"

"None yet."

"Even better."

"Hey," Michelle chimed loudly, "you two know the rules. No business discussions at the family breakfast."

"Who's talking business?" Marah questioned, looking across the room toward the table. "John Stallion, I know you did not bring up business at that breakfast table."

John's amusement gleamed in his wide smile. "Not me, baby," he said sheepishly.

Luke laughed, mumbling under his breath. "You are so busted!"

"Ain't that the truth." Matthew chuckled, as Mark laughed with them.

Marah and Eden placed platters of pancakes, bacon, scrambled eggs and assorted breakfast foods onto the table.

"We're ready to eat. Where did Daddy and Juanita disappear to?" Marla queried.

"Something about a tent," Luke responded. "I'll go get them," he volunteered, moving to his feet.

Matthew gestured for him to sit back down. "I'll do it. I have to take this call," he said, palming the cell phone that vibrated against his belt.

"No business!" the women all chimed in unison.

Matthew rolled his eyes as he moved toward the door and exited the room. Minutes later, Edward and Juanita strolled hand in hand into the space.

"Y'all need to set another plate," Edward chimed cheerily.

"Who's here, Daddy?" Eden queried.

"Miss Vanessa just pulled up outside. She and Matthew said they'd be here in a minute. Had something they needed to discuss."

"Hey, anyone else notice that those two have gotten

awful chummy lately?" Luke asked. His eyebrows were raised suggestively.

"Define chummy," Michelle said as she passed a plate of buttered toast.

"Didn't I just say that?" Mark said excitedly. "I told Mitch just the other day that there was something going on with those two. Didn't I say that, Mitch?"

Michelle nodded her head. "You did, honey."

"Oooh! Good gossip!" Marah exclaimed.

"Not at this table," Juanita interjected. "You all know better."

John laughed. "All of you act like there has to be something going on just because…what? The two are friends? Vanessa's been friends with us all since forever. There is nothing going on with her and Matthew."

"Well, it sure does look like something," Michelle said, gesturing toward the expansive picture window.

The whole family turned to stare where she pointed. Matthew and Vanessa stood toe to toe in deep conversation. Vanessa was clutching the front of Matthew's shirt with both palms. Exuberance filled her face as she stared up at the man, her awe-filled stare intense.

Juanita shook her head, moving over to the enclosure. She rapped her knuckles against the glass until she got their attention. When Matthew and Vanessa turned in her direction to see where the noise was coming from, she tossed up her hands, gesturing in the direction of the dining table.

Edward laughed. "I declare. If it's not one thing with you kids, it's something else."

Juanita's expression was scolding as she moved back to her seat. "If there is something going on, you all will scare them right from it. Leave 'em alone, and no teasing when they come in here, either."

"That's not fair, Aunt Juanita," Mark said. "If Vanessa is changing her ways, I want to be the first one to give her some static."

Juanita met his gaze, a reprimand at the tip of her tongue. She shifted that stare around the table. John stalled the admonishment with one of his own.

"I'm telling you people, it's nothing. Just let it drop before you make Matthew mad. You know how he gets when we tease him. He'll pout for days."

Mark chuckled. "Okay, if you say so. It's nothing."

"Oh, it's something!" Luke teased. "Y'all can act like you don't see it if you want to, but I know better."

Edward changed the subject. "Mitch, you done passed by the good food. I hope you ain't on one of them fool diets you young girls seem so fond of, 'cause this here is some good food."

Michelle shook her head as everyone turned their attention to her and her plate. "No, sir. I just haven't had much of an appetite lately. I think I might have picked up a mild stomach bug or something." She pushed at the fruit salad on her plate with her fork.

Marla tapped Marah on the leg, the two women cutting their eyes at each other. Across the table, Eden's eyebrows were raised sky high as she looked from one sister to the other.

"Baby, do you think you might be—" Juanita started before Matthew and Vanessa came into the room, their presence interrupting the conversation.

"Good morning!" Vanessa chimed. "How's everyone doing?"

Matthew moved back to the seat he'd vacated earlier. He ignored the looks his brothers were tossing him, their amused expressions shooting him quiet messages and silent questions.

Vanessa was still rambling as she took a seat at the other end of the table. "It sure pays to know where to find a good meal," she was saying as she reached for a platter of hotcakes. "And I'm famished!"

"Eat up, honey," Edward chuckled. "There's plenty to go around."

Luke laughed. "You people are too funny to me," he said, pulling a forkful of eggs into his mouth. "If y'all won't ask, I certainly will." He leaned forward, looking toward Matthew. Before he could fix his mouth to get the words out, Matthew interrupted him, stalling the query.

"So, Luke, have you found a date for the banquet yet?" he asked, his expression smug. Mischief shimmered in his gaze.

"Don't tell us you don't have a date yet, Luke," Marah intoned, her neck snapping as she turned to stare at him. "Luke, we have you confirmed as a party of two."

"And I know you didn't wait until the last minute to ask someone. Your date would have less than a day to find a dress," Marla added. "You know this is the biggest event in Dallas."

"Um, I have a date," Luke said, his voice dropping ever so slightly.

"Who? Someone you know well, we hope."

"You're not bringing one of your casual flings, are you?" Matthew asked, egging the situation on. "That really wouldn't be cool, bro."

Everyone's focus suddenly shifted to Luke.

Luke glared at Matthew, the man's smug stare reminiscent of when they'd been little and Luke had always gotten caught with his hand in the cookie jar, big brother giving his secrets away. In a fraction of a short second, Matthew had managed to put him under a microscope with the Briscoe-Stallion women biting at the bit to examine and dissect his personal life. His eyes widened in fright.

"You are bringing someone special, aren't you, baby?" Juanita asked.

"How about your friend Leslie?" Michelle queried. "She's very sweet."

"That girl Tanya would be good for you, too!" Vanessa chimed in with her two cents. "And she is way cute!"

"Really, guys, I have a date already. A very lovely young lady. I can't wait to introduce you all to her," he said, trying to sound convincing.

There was a quiet pause as the ladies studied him. John and Mark both burst out laughing. Matthew and the two men high-fived each other.

Marah shook her head. "Well, we hope so," she said finally. "This event is very important. And you know if you didn't have a date you could have let me and Eden know earlier. We could have fixed you up with a lovely escort for the night."

"And don't forget that you are confirmed for two," Juanita repeated.

Luke nodded as he dropped his eyes back into his plate. He pretended to be focused on the fried potatoes that topped his dish. Just like that, the conversation shifted again, Juanita putting Edward on the hot seat over something he'd forgotten to do.

As Luke's gaze moved around the table, he met Matthew's stare. His brother grinned, winking at him. Luke smiled back, chuckling softly to himself.

As he sat there, enjoying his family, his mind was racing a mile per minute. First thing on his agenda, he thought, was to find him a date before the sun set. He knew with total confidence who he wanted to ask, but went through the motion of mentally checking off his list of female friends. He was suddenly nervous, the short notice for the formal event being an issue.

This was a special event. This was truly a family affair. He couldn't ask just anyone to accompany him. He would much rather attend solo than have some casual acquaintance show up on his arm. As he ticked off name after name of possible dates, only one name kept surfacing to the top of the list. If anyone was special enough to fit the bill, she was, he thought as he reached for his cell phone. Suddenly Luke could only imagine himself celebrating the occasion with one woman. Joanne Lake.

Chapter 10

Joanne dropped her cell phone to the desktop. Her hand was shaking, nervous excitement rushing through her bloodstream. Luke Stallion's call had been an unexpected surprise and a very nice beginning to her day. Most especially after the previous evening they'd shared together.

The walk through the park had been a pleasant distraction. Joanne had needed that time to unwind, her nerves frayed from their encounter down at city hall. Neither she nor Luke had wanted that time to end as he had walked her slowly back to her car. Joanne drifted back into the moment.

"Can I interest you in dinner?" Luke had asked. His expression had been hopeful.

Joanne had glanced down to the watch on her wrist. "I don't want to impose on any more of your time."

"You wouldn't be imposing. I know this wonderful place—"

Joanne shook her head as she interrupted him, holding up her hand in pause. "Stop right there. I'm not flying anywhere. Not today."

The man laughed. "That's not a problem. We don't even have to leave downtown Dallas."

Her smile was wide and full. "I can do dinner, then."

Nodding his head, Luke gently tapped the side of her thigh, gesturing for her to slide over into the passenger seat. "If it's okay with you, I'll drive your car," he said, taking full control of the moment.

With her eyebrows raised ever so slightly, she tossed him a questioning look. Luke laughed warmly. "I'm just afraid that if I have you follow me you'll change your mind and turn around when we get there. So why don't you simply indulge me, relax and just let yourself have a good time? Okay?"

Shaking her head, Joanne giggled softly as she lifted her legs up and over the center console, sliding into the passenger seat. "I don't believe you," she said, the laugher radiating warmth over her face.

Their ride had taken less than twenty minutes. As they pulled into the driveway of Luke's Preston Hollow home, Joanne sensed that the man was better able to read her thoughts than she wanted to admit. He'd been right about her changing her mind. Had she been able, she would have turned her car around and raced back in the opposite direction. She couldn't begin to fathom what she had gotten herself into.

"Where are we?" Joanne questioned, her eyes dancing over the landscape. She hoped he couldn't see that she already knew the answer even before she'd asked it.

Luke smiled, his eyes shifting in her direction. "This is

my home. I thought we'd be able to sit back and relax, enjoy a good meal and just get to know each other better."

She nodded. "Well, this should be interesting."

Luke chuckled. "Very."

Minutes later, after a quick tour of the massive estate, Luke led her into the glass atrium that adorned the rear of the home. Joanne was immediately taken by the sheer beauty of the large Victorian conservatory. Drenched with light, the glass chamber looked out over the landscape outside, showcasing the wealth of flora that bloomed beautifully around them. The woman could feel herself falling into the moment, mesmerized by the magnitude of it all.

Luke was clearly amused by the expression that washed over her face, and he said so. "You are extraordinarily beautiful, Ms. Lake." He grazed his thumb lightly across the line of her profile.

Joanne could feel herself blush. "Thank you, Mr. Stallion," she answered softly.

Luke smiled, the brilliance of it hollowing deep dimples in his cheeks. "I hope you like peanut butter and jelly," he said, his expression serious as he changed the subject.

Laughter danced between them. "You're serious? Peanut butter and jelly?"

Luke nodded. "It's my best dish. I make a mean peanut butter and jelly sandwich."

Joanne returned the smile as she shrugged her shoulders. "Then peanut butter and jelly it will be," she said, dropping to the picnic blanket and floor cushions that rested at their feet. Luke held up an index finger, motioning for her to give him a quick minute.

Moving to the table on the other side of the room, Luke switched on the sound system, flooding the space with soft jazz. Returning to her side, he dropped down beside her, plates of sliced cheese and fruit in hand. A plastic container held wedges of finger sandwiches, rich homemade peanut butter and luscious strawberry jelly oozing from thick, freshly baked bread. A bottle of chilled champagne completed the meal.

As they savored the sweetness of fresh pineapple and polished off chunks of sweet mango, Joanne had lost all thought of the frustrations that had riddled their morning and afternoon. Pure joy had replaced the earlier anxiety that had consumed her. Every ounce of tension that had pulled across her shoulders had withered beneath the wealth of laughter the two had later shared. Joanne couldn't believe the good time she was having.

Luke nodded, as if reading her mind a second time. "This has been a lot of fun," he said, his gaze dancing with hers. "I'm glad we did this." The timbre of his voice was soft and warm, flooding her spirit. He reached for her hand, pulling the length of her fingers to his lips as he licked the fruit juices from their length. Joanne's eyes widened in surprise, a shudder of rising fervor heating her feminine spirit.

"I forgot the napkins," he said nonchalantly as if sliding his lips over her fingers were something he did every day.

Reaching for the last chocolate-covered strawberry, Luke had tilted it to her lips. Clasping her palm around his hand, she bit into the decadent fruit, savoring the sweetness of the dessert. Her tongue lightly grazed the tips of his fingers, and he smiled, temptation rising like a new day between them.

"Sweet," Luke muttered softly as he savored the last bite of strawberry. His gaze met Joanne's. She could feel her breath catch deep in her chest, and she held the oxygen for a second longer than necessary, afraid that if she breathed she might wake up and find that it had all just been a dream.

Her eyes skated across his face as she struggled not to stare back into the deep gaze he was giving her. She cleared her throat and lifted her body from where she sat. Moving to the windows, she stared out to the grounds outside. In the distance, the afternoon sun had begun to settle, a blanket of darkness being pulled up and over the land.

From where he still sat, Luke had stared after her. He chuckled softly to himself, intrigued by her efforts to ignore the rise of emotion sweeping between them. But there was no denying the rise of ardor that had been fueling the moment. Lifting his own body from the floor, Luke moved to stand where she stood, easing his body behind hers. As his chest pressed warmth against her back, he wrapped an arm around her waist, drawing the woman close against him.

Joanne had been amazed at how keenly they fit together, her body melding nicely against his. She closed her eyes, leaning back against his hard frame, and allowed herself to drop into the wealth of emotion that had consumed her. Luke's lips pressing a damp kiss against the back of her neck sent her desire into overdrive. She was suddenly conscious of his large palm kneading her midsection, his fingers dancing against her flesh. She struggled to suppress a moan that threatened to spill past her lips.

"I really should be going," Joanne said, stepping away from him. The heat from his hands still burned hot against her body.

Luke smiled. "You could stay," he said suggestively.

"That wouldn't be a good idea," she said. "And you need to get back to your car."

Luke laughed heartily, his head falling back against his

thick neck. "Here I was trying to seduce you, and all you can think about is getting me back to my car!"

Giggling, Joanne shook her head. "There will be no seducing here tonight. We need to call this evening to an end. I had a really nice time, though," she said, trying to sound convincing.

Luke stepped in closer, reaching for her hand. Holding it tightly he pressed a kiss into her palm. "Whatever you want, beautiful lady! Whatever you want!"

Color flushed Joanne's cheeks. "I had a very nice time tonight, Luke. Thank you."

Luke nodded. "That makes me very happy, Joanne. I had a great time, too," he said as he wrapped his arms back around her torso and hugged her tightly, wishing he didn't have to let her go.

Joanne heaved a deep sigh, inhaling air deep into her lungs. The memories of her evening were lingering hard and deep. Joanne's head was still swimming from the good time she'd had with the man. He'd been attentive and sweet, and each time he'd looked at her, she'd felt priceless. She didn't even want to begin to think about the many times that he'd touched her, his hand grazing the back of her hand or her forearm or resting lightly against the small of her back. Those times had left her wishing for something she had no business wanting. Joanne had gotten completely lost in the warmth of his touch.

She thought back to his arms being around her body as he'd hugged her good-night. Heat had risen between them with a fury that had left her speechless. She touched her arm where he'd last touched her, his fingers stroking her skin with complete abandon. The moment had taken her breath away. She shook her head, allowing the memories to sweep through her spirit.

* * *

What did I just do? Joanne thought suddenly, recalling his telephone call and the conversation the two had just shared minutes earlier. *What in the world was I thinking? I can't go out with that man again. I have to cancel!*

Joanne dropped her head into the palms of her hands. She couldn't begin to imagine how she'd allowed herself to get so caught up with how good the man had left her feeling. But Luke had left her feeling very good, and her good feeling had to do with the sensations that rose from his masculine presence when he was near.

Leaning back in her leather chair, Joanne crossed her arms over her chest, replaying their conversation over again in her head.

"Hey, Joanne, how are you?" Luke had asked, his voice like liquid gold in her ear, warm and seductive.

"Luke, hello!"

"I hope I'm not interrupting anything."

"No, not at all."

"I just wanted to tell you how much I enjoyed our time together last night."

"That's sweet of you. I had a very nice time, too."

"I was hoping we might be able to do it again. Sometime soon, maybe?"

There had been a moment's pause as Joanne had reflected on his comment. She was grinning into the telephone receiver when she finally responded. "I'd like that. I'd like that very much."

Luke's excitement was like static energy crossing the telephone line. "That's great. Is tomorrow night good for you?"

"Tomorrow? That's really soon!"

Luke chuckled. "Some people I know are having a small party tomorrow, and I would love it if you joined me."

"What kind of party?"

"Nothing major. Just a simple gathering of some friends and family. This will really be a group thing."

"Funny."

"So, you'll go?"

"Sure, why not."

"Great. This time I'll pick you up. The party starts at seven o'clock. I'll pick you up at six."

"I can just meet you."

"Really, it's not a problem. You live over by Fourth Street, right?"

Joanne's eyes had widened with surprise. "How did—?"

"Someone at the center mentioned it. What's your apartment number?"

Joanne had paused. She took a deep breath, gulping softly. "12-B."

"Great. I'll see you tomorrow. You have a great day, okay?"

"You, too," Joanne had said, her voice dropping to a loud whisper.

Before hanging up the phone, Luke had called her name. "Joanne?"

"Yes?"

"It's black tie. But I don't want you to worry about a dress. I'll have one delivered to you. Bye, Joanne."

Then he'd hung up. It had only taken her a New York minute after he'd disconnected the call to remember what was happening the following night: the Stallion banquet, which would kick off their annual rodeo event. Everyone was talking about it. Everyone who was anyone would be there.

The guest list was Dallas's elite and wealthy. Joanne had no doubts that if her father had been invited, the man would be there, front and center. There was absolutely no way she could go.

She dropped her hands into her palms a second time and pondered how she was going to get herself out of it.

She'd said yes! Luke was still tap dancing on cloud nine. His excitement didn't go unnoticed. Michelle cornered him on the rear lanai just as he'd flipped his cell phone closed.

"Found you a date, huh?"

The man laughed. "Was it that obvious?"

"The minute you said you had one," Michelle said, laughing with him, "you got this panicked look on your face. It wasn't pretty."

"Matthew thinks he's funny. Smart ass!"

"Oh, he was smart, all right. Your brother got you before you got him."

Luke chuckled again. "So, what's the skinny, Mitch? Is there something going on between him and Vanessa?"

The woman shrugged. "You're starting to sound like Mark now. I'm sure if those two want us to know something, they'll tell us."

Luke crossed his arms over his chest, leaning his back against the brick wall of the house. "So, when are you going to share your news?"

Michelle eyed him with reservation. "What news?"

"Don't play dumb now, Mitch Stallion. You know exactly what I'm talking about."

Michelle glanced over her shoulder, searching out the rest of the family. She clasped her arm through Luke's, pulling him beside her. "Walk with me." When they were some distance from the home, she turned to face him. "How did you know?"

"I don't know," he said facetiously. He held up his hand,

counting one finger at a time. "Maybe it's got something to do with the fact that you've been a strange shade of green for weeks now. You're only keeping every other meal down, and you're starting to lose your girlish figure. Except your boobs, of course—they've gotten huge!"

Michelle threw a punch, hammering Luke against the shoulder. Luke laughed as he rubbed at the bruise she'd inflicted.

"So, I'm right. You are pregnant!"

"Don't you dare tell Mark! I want to surprise him at the anniversary celebration."

Luke wrapped an arm around her shoulder, hugging her close. "He won't hear it from me, but you know how the rest of these Stallions are. Not one of them can keep a secret. And if I figured it out, I know they have. In case you didn't catch it, Aunt Juanita was just about to out your secret back there."

"I know. I've been dodging questions from her and Marah all morning." Michelle smiled, shaking her head. "I swear, I think Mark is still the only one who doesn't have a clue, and the man wakes up with me every morning." She pressed her palms to her abdomen.

Luke smiled down on her. "He's going to be thrilled. Don't you worry. I am so excited for both of you. Wow, I'm going to be an uncle!"

"Double wow! I'm going to be a mother."

"You and Mark will make wonderful parents. I'm sure you two will have little Junior riding a Harley home from the hospital."

Michelle giggled as their names were called to draw their attention to the other side of the property. Mark was gesturing for them to come back.

Michelle bumped her shoulder against Luke's arm. "You

promised, so don't fail me. After tomorrow night, it won't be a secret anymore."

Pretending to zipper his lips, Luke smiled. "No problem, but I really need you to do me one big favor in return."

"What's that?"

"What do you know about buying a ball gown?"

History painted the walls of the home's library. The décor was a collage of family images, framed civic awards, trophies and books. Books filled shelves that ran from the floor to the ceiling along two walls. The ambiance was warming, the dark wood of the bookcases against taupe walls creating a place that felt secure and inviting.

Edward sat in one of four leather chairs, listening intently to John as he gave him an update on their business activities. The mood was somber, their expressions too serious for comfort.

"How bad is it?" Edward asked, his hands clasped tightly together in his lap.

John met his gaze. He took a deep lungful of air, blowing it slowly past his lips before he responded. "It's not good, Edward. It's not good at all.

"Fill me in, son."

"Six months ago, a representative from E-Kal Industries approached me with an offer to purchase the company. I took the initial meetings to see what they were proposing but I had no serious intentions of selling my business, and I told them so. I have to admit, though, it was an impressive offer. Very impressive. But I turned it down.

"Since then, someone's been buying up some significant Stallion stock. All of our major stockholders have been approached about selling, and some of them actually have. Now, word on the grapevine is that neither I nor our current management team is acting in the best interest of the shareholders…"

"Opening the door for a proxy fight if they can convince enough of the shareholders to go along with it," Edward finished for him.

John nodded. "Yes. For the time being, Mark and I are meeting with as many of the shareholders as we can to reassure them that there is nothing they need to be concerned about. And Matthew's got a team researching E-Kal. We need to know who's behind this."

Edward heaved a deep sigh, leaning back in his chair. He nodded his gray head. "What can I do to help?"

The younger man shook his head, leaning forward as he rested his elbows on top of his legs and dropping his head into his hands. "You're doing it, Edward. I appreciate your support. I have to tell you, I've only been scared a few times in my life, and this has got me scared." John raised his eyes to meet Edward's intense stare. "Really scared. I can't fail this family. I can't."

Matthew held the home's front door open as Vanessa stepped past him to the front porch. Stepping out behind her, Matthew pushed his hands deep into the pockets of his khaki slacks. The duo traversed the steps down to the driveway, coming to stand beside Vanessa's motorcycle. She unlatched her helmet from its resting place, pulled it onto her head and affixed the strap beneath her chin. Matthew finally broke the silence between them.

"Vanessa, are you certain about this? I mean, really certain that this is what you want?"

She gave him a bright smile, her head nodding in assent. "More than you will ever know."

Matthew blew a deep sigh. "Well, neither of us is going to be able to keep it a secret much longer. They're already asking questions," he said, gesturing toward the house. "You know how my brothers can get."

Vanessa chuckled as she leaned up to kiss his cheek. Reaching for his hand, she squeezed it tightly, holding it beneath her own. "I know, but I couldn't do this without you, Matthew. I trust your judgment. You don't know how much it means to me to have you supporting me."

"Vanessa, you know I'd never abandon you."

"I know. That's why I love you so much." She squeezed his hand a second time before swinging her leg over the bike, adjusting her body against the narrow seat.

Matthew shook his head. "We need to talk about you riding this bike, Vanessa. I'm fairly certain it's not good for the baby."

Vanessa laughed. "The kid's got to learn to ride sooner or later. Besides, I'll give it up when I get too big to ride. Don't you worry."

"Well, I do worry, and when the family finds out, they're going to worry, too."

Vanessa rolled her eyes. "I hear you talking, Daddy," she said as she started her engine.

Matthew shook his head. "Just be safe," he said as she wheeled herself back just enough to disengage the kickstand. "And keep Junior safe, too."

Winking, Vanessa grinned widely and then was riding down the driveway and back through the gates.

Chapter 11

The three women stood staring at the large white box that had been delivered just minutes before. Marley's mother, Estelle Brooks, stood with her hands on her hips, shaking her head vehemently as she chastised Joanne.

"So when you gon' tell this boy the truth? This don't make no kind of sense, Joanne. No kind of sense at all. Got this boy thinking you live here when you got that nice condominium your daddy paid good money for. And why you give him this address anyway? No kind of sense!"

Joanne cut her eyes toward Marley, who was grinning like a Cheshire cat. She was hoping for a little assistance but knew none was coming. Both women had learned years ago that when Estelle Brooks went off on a tangent about something, then that something was going to be the topic of discussion for many discussions to come. Staying out of the line of fire was the best recourse, if you knew what was good for you.

An Important Message from the Publisher

Dear Reader,

Because you've chosen to read one of our fine novels, I'd like to say "thank you"! And, as a special way to say thank you, I'm offering to send you two more Kimani™ Romance novels and two surprise gifts – absolutely FREE! These books will keep it real with true-to-life African American characters that turn up the heat and sizzle with passion.

Please enjoy the free books and gifts with our compliments...

Glenda Howard

For Kimani Press

Peel off Seal and Place Inside...

We'd like to send you two free books to introduce you to Kimani™ Romance books. These novels feature strong, sexy women, and African-American heroes that are charming, loving and true. Our authors fill each page with exceptional dialogue, exciting plot twists, and enough sizzling romance to keep you riveted until the very end!

KIMANI ROMANCE ... LOVE'S ULTIMATE DESTINATION

Your two books have a combined cover price of $13.98, but are yours **FREE!** We'll even send you two wonderf surprise gifts. You can't lose!

The Reader Service — Here's How It Works:

BUSINESS REPLY MAIL
FIRST-CLASS MAIL   PERMIT NO. 717   BUFFALO, NY

POSTAGE WILL BE PAID BY ADDRESSEE

THE READER SERVICE
PO BOX 1867
BUFFALO NY 14240-9952

NO POSTAGE
NECESSARY
IF MAILED
IN THE
UNITED STATES

The older woman finally took a breath, stalling long enough to inhale and allow Joanne to try to defend herself.

"I really didn't lie to him, Mama Estelle. He just assumed you were my mother and that I lived here with you, and I just didn't correct him."

"No kind of sense!"

Joanne didn't have a response to that, knowing that the older woman was right. Estelle Brooks usually was. Joanne had been six years old the day Marley and her mom had come into her life. The woman had been the last of a long list of housekeepers hired to maintain the Lake homestead and keep an eye on the precocious Joanne. The familial bond between them had been solidified when the two girls had gotten into a knock-down, drag-out fight over a pair of plastic pumps for a Barbie doll.

After separating the two, Estelle had taken a carving knife to Barbie, separating her right down the middle. Each girl had gotten half a doll and one plastic shoe each. The absurdity of the action had left both girls in a fit of giggles. It took no time at all for them to discover that if they didn't share and play fair, Mama Estelle would make them share the hard way. A month of toys, some Joanne's and some Marley's, had been sacrificed for the lesson.

Eventually the two girls were inseparable, both gaining something the other yearned for. Estelle filled Joanne's bill for a full-time, surrogate mother, and Joanne's father became an adequate part-time dad for Marley.

Estelle Brooks had helped Joanne navigate her first bra, first period, first bad haircut and first heartbreak and had mothered her for the forty-six weeks of each year that Joanne resided stateside with her father.

"Mama Estelle, what else could I do? He doesn't know about my father."

"So tell him. Are you ashamed of your father, Joanne?"

"No, it's not that. It's just…well…" Joanne paused.

"She's ashamed of her father's money," Marley said matter-of-factly.

"No, I'm not. I'm ashamed of how my father flaunts his money."

"That's sheer nonsense," Estelle said, flipping her hand in Joanne's direction. "Isn't this boy wealthy?"

"Filthy rich!" Marley chimed.

Joanne shook her head, rolling her eyes skyward. "This isn't about his money or mine. When people find out Charles Lake is my father, they don't take me seriously. Everyone automatically assumes that I'm this spoiled and pampered princess. They treat me differently. I want Luke to get to know me without judging me solely on my father's wealth and status!"

"Did you judge him on his wealth and status?" Estelle asked, eyebrows raised.

"She sure did," Marley interjected.

Joanne glared at her best friend.

"I don't understand you, Joanne. Since you was a little girl you'd rather be here in the projects with me and Marley than at your own home. Your daddy has tried to raise you with the best of everything, and not one bit of it has made you comfortable or happy." Estelle shook her head. "I swear, it don't make no kind of good sense!"

The woman moved toward the bed and the oversized box that rested there. She pulled at a white envelope that was secured to the top. "What's it say?" she queried as she passed it to Joanne.

Joanne fingered the envelope momentarily before pulling the handwritten note card from inside. Luke's bold signature stared up at her, his handwriting neat and precise. She read the sweet message aloud.

"Hey, Joanne!—Thank you for saving me from a night of loneliness. Hope you like my selection. I thought it would be stunning on you. Can't wait to see your beautiful smile again. Luke"

Marley crossed her arms over her chest, humming softly. "Hmm…"

Joanne's mouth fell open as Estelle and her daughter pulled the gorgeous gown from the box. The silk design was a strapless bodice with a shirred waist that fell into a billowy, floor-length skirt. The top was lined with built-in support so the wearer didn't have need for any intimate apparel. The shirring was situated to define any waistline. But it was the color that grabbed full attention, the silk fabric a vibrant shade of brilliant, jaw-dropping red.

"Oh, my God. It's gorgeous!" Marley exclaimed excitedly.

"What size is it?" Joanne asked, hopeful that it being too small might be the excuse she needed to pass on the event.

Marley eyed the tag stitched into the back of the dress. "Your size!" she said excitedly.

Joanne reached a hand out to caress the richness of the fabric. She groaned loudly.

"What is wrong with you?" Estelle asked, annoyance rising in her voice.

"I can't go. What if my father is there?"

"So what if he is?"

"I don't want Luke to find out about my father that way. I want to tell him first so that I can explain why I didn't tell him in the beginning."

Estelle shook her head. She reached for the telephone on the nightstand, pulling the receiver into her hand as she dialed.

Both Joanne and Marley exchanged a look between them as they stared at the woman curiously.

"Hello, Mrs. Deavers? Estelle Brooks here. How are you, dear?" The woman paused. "And that handsome son of yours?" She paused again. "So glad to hear it."

Joanne focused on the one side of the conversation Estelle was having with her father's personal secretary.

"My girl is doing good. Still home, still going to school. Hope to marry her off one day, so if you ever want to arrange something with your son…" The woman chortled, making a face at Marley as she did. "Honey, can you tell me if Dr. Lake is going to that Stallion party tonight?… Really?…You don't say…My, my, my…" There was a long moment of silence as Estelle listened intently to the woman on the other end. Every so often she would cluck her teeth or mutter. "Honey, hush your mouth!" she exclaimed loudly, laughing again. "Well, you take care, dear, and I certainly appreciate that information."

After hanging up the receiver, Estelle grinned. "Your daddy is in New York. He declined the Stallion invitation."

Joanne could feel her own wide smile pulling at her mouth. Estelle lifted the dress from the bed, moving to hang it against the closet door. Heading out of the small room, she called out Joanne's name.

"Yes, ma'am?"

"Since you pretending this is your home, you need to pretend them dirty dishes right out of that kitchen sink. Then you need to pretend that dust out of the living room and vacuum them floors before that boy gets here."

Marley burst out laughing.

Joanne could only shake her head. "Yes, ma'am."

Hours later, Joanne stood staring at herself in the full-length mirror in Marley's small bedroom. The woman staring back at her was gorgeous. The dress Luke had chosen fit her figure to a T. The design flattered her hills and accentuated her valleys. The color shimmered against her warm complexion, creating a stunning view.

Marley had done her hair, using the smallest of curling irons imaginable to sweep her short do into a wealth of curls. Her makeup was old Hollywood glamorous, with her black eyeliner and ruby red lipstick. Mama Estelle had loaned her a pair of pearl earrings, the simple teardrop setting adorning her ears.

Joanne was still awed by the fact that she was actually going to do a formal evening with the likes of Luke Stallion. The chores had taken most of the afternoon, dishes and dusting expanding to window washing and a host of other small to-dos that Estelle had thought of. When Joanne had begun to think that she would never get finished, Marley had extended a helping hand, teasing her the entire time.

Immediately after laying down her cleaning supplies, Joanne had managed to lounge for a brief moment in a hot tub of bubbles to ease her tension away. Marley had sat atop the closed commode, the two women giggling at Estelle's life lesson as if they were six years old again.

Standing there in the mirror, Joanne was still trying to decide if she'd made the right choice. Before she could change her mind, Marley was screaming about a limousine, and Luke Stallion was pulling up outside in front of the building.

Luke lifted himself from the stretch Escalade. Looking around, he took in his surroundings. The brick units were well aged, most having seen better days and more maintenance. The outsides were blacktop and gravel, no grass or trees, and only a spattering of planters situated with living plant life in front of a few doors in desperate need of a coat of paint.

Neighbors sitting on well-worn chairs eyed him suspiciously as children darted back and forth around the car. Across the parking lot, a group of young men were playing basketball beneath a hoop that had no net. Another group leaned against the back of an old Buick Riviera, looking like they were clearly up to no good. Everyone was staring to see the man who'd come knocking on Miss Estelle's front door.

Luke suddenly thought about his conversation with Michelle as she'd helped him shop for a dress. Michelle had shared that she'd been a little anxious when she'd first met the Stallion family. Her first date with Mark had been over the top, the man jetting her clear across the country for a lavish weekend away. For a woman who'd grown up more modestly, Michelle admitted it had been overwhelming, taking her some time to get used to. Luke had told her about his conversations with Joanne, and his sister-in-law had mused that perhaps Joanne was intimidated by a lifestyle she'd never experienced before.

Luke was suddenly determined to ease her discomfort. He wanted her to share his experiences and hoped that she might be more willing to share her own with him. He pushed the doorbell and then waited patiently for someone to answer.

Joanne could hear them in the living room, Mama Estelle welcoming the man inside. She was only slightly fearful that the woman would give her away, but since Mama Estelle always referred to both girls as her babies and she and Marley always introduced themselves as sisters,

Joanne felt fairly confident it would go well without any of them having to tell a blatant lie. She could hear Luke's warm laugh as she made her way out of the room.

His eyes widened noticeably when she stepped into the room, his gaze drinking her in like a man dying of thirst. Joanne bowed her head in greeting, her own stare focused on how dashing he looked in his formal wear. The designer tuxedo fit him meticulously, with its single-button, single-breasted satin notch and self-topped collar. His vest and matching tie were the same shade as her gown, matching it perfectly. Joanne knew beyond any doubt that pulling that off with one day's notice hadn't been easy, or cheap.

"You take my breath away," Luke said, his voice a deep whisper as he took two steps toward her, meeting her in the center of the room.

Joanne smiled, a current of electricity flooding her senses as he clasped her hands beneath his, leaning in to press a light kiss to her cheek.

"Thank you. The dress is beautiful, but you really shouldn't have."

Luke shook his head. "Yes, I should have. You are absolutely beautiful in that dress."

From the corner of her eye, Joanne could see Marley and Estelle watching them with amusement. "Have you met Mama Estelle and Marley?" she asked, tossing them both a quick look.

Luke nodded. "Yes, we were just getting to know one another."

"Yes, we was." Estelle chuckled. "You two stand there so I can get me a picture. Marley, baby, take Joanne's picture with her young man, please."

"Yes, ma'am," Marley answered, focusing the digital camera.

Joanne felt a shiver glide the length of her spine as Luke

wrapped an arm around her waist, his large palm coming to rest against the small of her back as he struck a pose beside her. The man's confidence was engaging, the energy of it radiating from his body. Beside him, Joanne suddenly felt out of her element, certain that she had to look like a deer caught in headlights when Marley snapped the picture.

Chapter 12

Joanne rolled from one side of the king-size bed to the other, her hand brushing against the empty spot Luke Stallion had occupied just hours earlier. A wide smile pulled full across her face. She still couldn't believe the last twelve hours had actually happened to her. She would gladly roll back the clock and do it all over again, she thought. She curled her body around an oversized pillow, hugging it tightly as she drifted back into the memories.

It hadn't taken a rocket scientist to tell her that Mama Estelle and Marley both had been impressed with Luke. The man had taken a seat on Mama Estelle's plastic-covered furniture, making himself comfortable in her living room. Without blinking an eye, he had the matriarch telling him about her family, her ties to Dallas and some secrets even she and Marley had never been privy to.

As the couple had headed out the door, Mama Estelle was still giggling like a teenager. Joanne couldn't wait until she and her surrogate family were together again so that she and Marley could tease the woman.

The ride to the Briscoe Ranch had set the tone for the evening. Luke had been engaging, his easygoing nature making her quite comfortable in his presence. He had talked about his brothers and their wives, the pride for his family gleaming in his eyes. His excitement fueled her own, washing away the hint of anxiety that teased her senses. Her earlier reservations had dissipated into thin air, and Joanne could feel herself having a good time, enjoying the man and his company.

It wasn't until the limousine pulled into the large estate, winding its way around to the banquet facility that Joanne had suddenly felt another quiver of apprehension prickle her insides. Only then did she start to question for the umpteenth time if she should even be there. Stepping out of the limo, Luke had grabbed her hand, entwining her fingers between his, and he held it like he'd been holding her hand all her life. Squeezing it gently as he'd smiled down at her, Joanne sensed that he wouldn't let her go, that Luke Stallion would hold on to her for as long as she needed him to. Any angst she'd been feeling was gone as quickly as it had risen.

Their entrance did not go unnoticed. Before they'd gotten into the room good, his family had surrounded them, the introductions fast and furious. His sister-in-law Michelle had hugged Joanne warmly, whispering in her ear that she shouldn't be nervous. Juanita Briscoe and her husband had been as gracious, making her feel exceptionally welcome. And his brothers had been engaging, the three beautiful black men standing tall and impressive in the tuxedos that fit them like well-made gloves. They'd given her the once-over and him a nod of approval. Their good-natured teasing about their younger sibling having arrived, and not alone, had made her smile, and for a brief moment it had made her laugh to see Luke standing uncomfortable under the scrutiny.

It had been an exceptionally long time since Joanne had attended such a formal event. As she'd scanned the room knowing that Luke would want to introduce her to his friends and business associates, she couldn't help but fear that someone would recognize her or know her father. The expression on her face was disconcerting, and Luke had noticed and had sought to ease her discomfort.

"Hey, buddy, do you want leave?" he'd asked.

Joanne's look had been incredulous. "We can't do that."

Luke had chuckled. "We can do whatever we want. We've made our appearance, said our hellos. Now let's go have some real fun."

And just like that they were back in the limousine headed back to downtown Dallas.

"What do you like to do for entertainment?" Luke had asked.

Joanne had chuckled softly. "Who has time for entertainment? Work takes up all of my time, and the center takes up whatever is left."

Luke shook his head. "There must be something you like to do for fun. What's the last thing you did that was the best time you'd ever had? And our date the other night doesn't count," he said, his eyebrows raised ever so slightly.

Joanne had thought for a brief moment, one evening in time standing out in her memory. "Bowling," she'd answered, laughter flooding her spirit as she'd told him about one of her weekend excursions with Marley. "It was like we were kids again. We went bowling and to the movies and it was the best time," she'd exclaimed excitedly.

Luke had nodded his head, a sly smile on his face, and

within minutes they were pulling on matching red, white and blue bowling shoes with her formal gown and his tuxedo. Joanne had never laughed so hard in her life, the two of them drawing much attention to their absurdity.

From the bowling alley they'd gone to a small burger joint for a meal of grilled hamburgers laden with lettuce, tomatoes and extra cheese and a side of onion rings and two super-thick strawberry milkshakes. Joanne smiled as she remembered the laughter that rang so soundly between them, both of them thoroughly enjoying each other's company.

She'd felt exceptionally comfortable with him, Luke moving her to expose more of herself than she'd shared with any man before. The conversation had flowed easily as they'd navigated one subject after another. Both of them had been taken aback by the level of ease they found with each other, and Joanne and Luke both were suddenly imagining where their new-found friendship could take them.

From the small diner, they'd moved to the movie theater. A debate had been waged at the ticket window, Joanne wanting to see the newest Will Smith movie and Luke more excited by some shoot-'em-up action flick. Joanne and Will Smith won the battle. The young girl at the counter had told them how cute they were together, making her blush profusely as Luke had agreed, gripping her by the shoulder as he'd casually leaned to kiss her cheek.

By the time they'd purchased their tickets, a large bucket of buttered popcorn and a gigantic box of Jordan Almonds, Joanne was floating on air. She couldn't remember the last time she'd had so much fun with a man who was clearly having a wonderful time with her.

The late-night viewing had been completely empty, the two having the theater all to themselves as they'd sat at the uppermost level of the theater beneath the movie projection booth. They'd propped their legs against the back of the seats in front of them as he'd held the bucket of popcorn between them.

Mid-movie, Luke had slipped an arm around her shoulder, pulling her close. The move was smooth as he'd stretched out both arms, pretending to yawn, then letting his right arm drop easily behind her back while his left hand had lifted away the chair arm between them. The gesture had made Joanne laugh.

"That was slick," she'd said with a warm giggle.

"I know," he'd responded, winking at her. "I'm good like that."

Beneath the veil of darkness she'd leaned into his side, allowing herself to relax against him, enjoying the rise of body heat between them. Then Luke had softly nuzzled her neck, pressing light kisses along the length of her jawline, and Joanne felt her composure weakening.

"Thank you," Luke had whispered into her ear, warm breath teasing her skin.

"For what?" Joanne had whispered back, fighting to maintain her decorum as she feigned interest in the movie screen before them.

"For the best night of my whole life."

Joanne had grinned broadly, the wide smile filling her face as Luke had smiled back. His next question had only taken her by surprise for a brief second before she was nodding her assent.

"May I kiss you, Joanne?" he'd asked, leaning his face close to hers, his warm breath blowing waves of anticipation through her.

When he'd covered her mouth with his own, Joanne had known there would be no turning back. Clasping her face between his hands, his kiss had been heated and searching, his lips moving hungrily over hers. It was as if there were not enough of her to kiss. Joanne had returned Luke's fervor with her own, opening herself to his invading tongue. She'd licked and sucked at his full lips, savoring his mouth with full appreciation. The abandon they were both showing proved to be a powerful aphrodisiac.

Luke had pulled away from her, staring down into her eyes. "We can't be friends anymore," he'd gasped, his voice deep and husky.

Confusion had washed over Joanne's expression. "Why? I don't—"

"Because I really want to make love to you, and if you tell me you don't make love to your friends, I'm going to be devastated," he'd said with a sly smile.

Joanne had laughed, and then he'd kissed her again, shifting his body in his seat to pull her against him. His tongue left her mouth and trailed a heated path down her chin and onto her delicate neck. He'd nibbled at her flesh until she'd heard herself moaning and cooing softly in his arms. Kisses had rained like water, a torrential wave of heat and passion rising out of nowhere. Before either of them knew it, the credits were rolling across the massive movie screen, the house lights rising softly in the room.

Neither of them could keep their hands off the other as they had sat in the back of the limousine, the SUV gliding nowhere through the streets of Dallas. Her beautiful dress was suddenly in the way as Luke slipped a large palm beneath the hem, drawing warm caresses against her bare legs. Joanne had pressed her hands to his chest, pulling at the white dress shirt that separated her touch from his flesh.

In one swift move, Luke had lifted her from her seat, pulling her into his lap. Joanne had slipped her arms around his neck, their mouths still locked together. Luke had groaned as he'd pulled at the zipper to her dress, pushing the top of the silk garment down toward her waist. Sliding his hands over her naked back, his fingers ignited every nerve ending through Joanne's body as he caressed the bare skin of her shoulders and back, tracing a path down to her full waist and crest of her buttocks. She'd suddenly wanted him with a fervor she'd never known for any man before.

Breaking the kiss, Luke had stared into her eyes, desire smoldering in his own dark orbs. In that moment, both of them had no reservations about what they were craving. Luke had wanted her with every fiber of his being. His eyes wide with appreciation, he'd gently cupped her large breasts in both palms, gently exploring the chocolate peaks. Cradling his head against her chest, his mouth slid wetly over her nipples as he'd suckled one and then the other, his tongue lashing at the lush buttons that had hardened like rock candy at his touch.

Joanne had squirmed against him. The sensation of his lips latched around her flesh, sucking her in, had sent tendrils of pleasure through the core of her body. She'd threaded her fingers across the low-cropped cut of his hair, pulling him closer to her. Throwing her head back against her neck, Joanne had moaned, a hiss of pleasure filling the midnight air.

Luke had kneaded the flesh between his lips, savoring the silkiness of her skin, the hardness of her nipple on his tongue. Pleasuring her was all he could think of, was all he wanted, as Joanne rocked against his lap, giving in to her carnal desires. He could feel her heat pulsing through the fabric of her skirt, igniting a pounding through his lower extremities. He'd suddenly been consumed with tasting every square inch of her body.

"If you want me to stop, you need to tell me now," Luke

whispered, his voice husky with desire. "Tell me now, baby, before we take this any further."

Joanne had pulled back to stare into his face, meeting his intense gaze with one of her own. There was no denying the rush of emotions sweeping through them both. Stopping him was the last thing on her mind as his hands skated across her thighs.

"Make love to me," she said out loud, leaning back to capture his mouth with her own, kissing him eagerly.

With those words, Luke gently eased his large hand beneath Joanne's thighs, pressing two fingers against the entrance of that sweet spot between her legs. She gasped loudly at his touch, her expression expectant and crazed with lust as he eased his fingers beneath her panties. His digits were slowly swallowed up by the hot, tight, velvet sheath of her body. Both of them moaned loudly as every lingering inhibition about where they were and what they were doing was thrown to the wind.

"Oh, yessss," Joanne hissed. She slowly began to rock her hips back and forth, her body clutching and clenching the man's fingers.

With his free hand, Luke grabbed her buttocks, gripping a cheek as she shamelessly drove herself up and down against him. Her breath was coming in sharp gasps as she moaned his name over and over again, the sweetness of the chant like music to his ears.

Luke had watched as Joanne had rotated her hips against his hand. Her body was lush and full, the suppleness of her pelvis enough to rival the most seasoned athlete. Perspiration dampened her skin, glistening like gold against her complexion. She was beautiful, and he wanted her more than he'd ever wanted any woman before her.

With wild abandon, Joanne had moved faster, her hips becoming a blur against him. Luke moved to steady her against his lap. Understanding that she was at a point of no return, he opened his mouth and quickly drew one of the large breasts past his lips. He swirled his tongue around the plump fullness, grazing the hardened nipple with the edge of his teeth. When he did, Joanne had thrown back her head and screamed.

Incomprehensible words of lust had spilled from her mouth, and then she'd bucked her body skyward as an orgasm ripped through her. Her body had shuddered and thrashed in his arms, her private chamber clutching his fingers even tighter. And then she fell forward against him, gasping heavily for air.

As her breathing normalized, Joanne had stared at him, her curls tangled, her dress wrinkled. Her gaze had been just shy of vacant, her lips swollen from his kisses, her face flushed. She'd been beautiful, and Luke had said so. Leaning his face against hers, Luke had chuckled softly, whispering into her ear. "Foreplay has officially begun."

Remembering, Joanne now quivered against the mattress. The man hadn't been teasing. It had been the beginning, and what followed had left her body aching delightfully with pure, unadulterated pleasure.

Luke was shaking his head. No one was saying anything, his brothers all silent to keep the attention diverted away from them. Luke was under attack—not one of the women in the family happy with him.

He cut his eye toward John, his gaze pleading for some assistance. John turned his eyes to the other side of the room, a smug smile hidden behind a copy of *Fortune* magazine.

Sighing, Luke knew he was on his own, no help coming from any of the male members of their family.

Marah had just stopped berating him when Juanita

picked up the rant. "I just don't understand it, Luke Stallion. You weren't there for ten minutes. You walked in and barely bothered to introduce your young lady to your family before you were dragging the poor thing out the door!"

"Did you get an introduction?" Marah queried. "Because I never got to meet the woman."

"Her gown was gorgeous," Michelle interjected, a wry smile pulling at her mouth.

"Wasn't it pretty!" Marla exclaimed. "And she was so sweet."

"And you didn't take one picture!" Juanita chimed. "Not one of the family pictures is going to have you two in it. What did you think, Luke? That we hired that expensive photographer for the fun of it?"

There was a moment of thundering silence as the women stood staring down at him, hands clutching hips with vague irritation. Luke looked from one to the other, realizing that their silence was the signal that they were waiting for an explanation. They wanted Luke to make sense of what they didn't understand.

Before Luke could think to respond, Edward became the voice of reason. "I swear, you women are like a pack of wolves." He turned to face Luke. "Luke, did you have a good time with your lady friend, son?"

Luke nodded, a flash of memory flooding his bloodstream. He cleared his throat, trying not to let the emotions get away from him. "Yes, sir. We had a terrific time together."

"Then that's all that matters. Y'all leave this boy alone!"

The other men burst out laughing.

"Well, I don't think it's very funny. Not at all," Marah concluded.

Juanita was still shaking her index finger at him. "And

you missed Mark and Mitch's announcement. They're going to have a baby!"

Luke grinned, leaning over to pound fists with Mark. He winked at Michelle.

"That's not the announcement he missed," Mark chuckled under his breath.

Luke looked confused. "What? What else did I miss?"

"Yeah, tell him what he missed, Matthew," John chimed.

Matthew rolled his eyes. "Vanessa's expecting a baby, too."

Wide-eyed, Luke stared at Matthew with his mouth hanging open. "Vanessa? How?"

Mark laughed. "I thought John explained how babies were made when you were twelve?"

"And I explained it to you again just last year," Matthew teased.

Luke flipped a dismissive hand at both of them. "Who's the father?" Luke asked, looking at Matthew a second time.

The whole room seemed to lean forward at the same time, anticipation waiting for Matthew to answer.

A bemused expression washed over Matthew's face, but he said nothing, only shrugging his shoulders.

"We only found out by accident," Mark said. "It seems Vanessa wasn't quite ready for us to know anything."

"And we're all going to respect her privacy," Juanita interjected. "I'm sure whoever that baby's daddy is, he'll do right by it and by Vanessa," she said as she moved past Matthew's chair and tapped the back of his head.

"Ouch! What was that for?" Matthew exclaimed, rubbing at the back of his skull.

"Just a love tap," Juanita said matter-of-factly.

John, Mark and Luke laughed warmly, all of them remembering many a love tap inflicted by Juanita.

Luke leaned forward to stare at his brothers. "Well, I only have one question. Does this mean Vanessa's not a lesbian anymore?"

Chapter 13

Sneaking away from his family, Luke retreated to the front porch to call Joanne. He wanted to make sure the driver had gotten her home safely. He also wanted to invite her back to the ranch for some of the rodeo events. Most important of all, though, Luke wanted to tell the exquisite woman that he was already missing her.

And he was. Leaving Joanne's side that morning had taken more than he had expected. She'd been sleeping peacefully in his arms, her back cushioned against his naked torso, and he'd been enamored with just how neatly they fit together. If he had his way, he would still be with her, still holding her, but his familial responsibilities had required his time and attention.

Luke heaved a deep sigh. Their high school petting had gone from the theater to the rear of the limo. Touching her had been all he'd wanted to do. Everything else had been a bonus he'd not expected. He smiled a wicked smile as he recalled their late-night rendezvous.

He had ignored the cell phone vibrating in the breast pocket of his tuxedo jacket. He'd also ignored the buzz from the driver seated at the front of the vehicle. All he'd been focused on was bringing Joanne pleasure. Clearly spent from his initial ministrations, Joanne's eyes had widened with intrigue when he'd whispered that foreplay had officially begun.

Reaching for his cell phone he'd placed a quick call, securing a room at the Ritz-Carlton. Then he'd sent the driver in that direction as he'd helped Joanne readjust her clothes. She'd giggled when he'd noted that doing so was a complete waste of time, since he fully intended to have her out of them by the time they made it up to their hotel room. Color had risen to her round cheeks as she'd blushed at the implications.

Stepping out of the limo, his hands were still holding her, his arm wrapped protectively around her waist as he guided her up to the penthouse suite. He'd been half right about having her out of her clothes before reaching their room.

The elevator doors had barely closed, securing them in the conveyor, before Luke had dropped to his knees before her. Reaching beneath her dress he'd grasped her lace panties and tugged them down toward her knees. Joanne had inhaled swiftly as he'd gestured for her to step out of the silk garment.

Pressing lace and silk to his face, he'd inhaled her sweet aroma, his eyes widening with anticipation as he gazed up at her. The look was sultry, burning hot through Joanne's spirit. Instinct moved her to lift the skirt of her dress to her waist, exposing herself fully.

Smiling, Luke reached behind him, pushing the

elevator's Stop button. Joanne's smile melted with his as the conveyor came to a quick halt somewhere between the fifteenth and sixteenth floors.

Taking his hands, Joanne had guided them over her abdomen and across her hips, directing him to gently stroke the building ache that was rising with her desire. Luke could feel the heat drawing him to the door of her satin crevice. Widening her thighs to give him access to the moist petals, Joanne groaned as Luke probed her opening, stroking the slippery wetness of her excitement.

"Oh, Luke!" she'd cried as he'd fondled the soft, delicate flesh, his fingers darting into her with ease.

But touching her hadn't been enough. Luke had yearned for more. Clasping her behind the cushion of her thighs, he'd moved his head between them. When his tongue had lapped at her hungrily, Joanne lost all control. Biting her lip, her breath came in a heated, gasping rhythm. She moaned deep in her throat as Luke continued to flick the tip of his tongue over her feminine spirit.

Joanne was a sweet delicacy, the appetizer before what would prove to be a very satisfying meal. Luke savored the taste of her as he sampled her slowly, appreciating the nuances of her taste, her texture and the maddening scent that had him rock hard in his slacks.

The elevator resuming its trek upward was the only thing that had stalled him from bringing her to orgasm a second time. The unexpected shake of the enclosure moved Luke to come to his feet. Pulling down her dress, the man had stuffed her panties into his jacket pocket just before pulling her into another heated embrace, his mouth locking with hers.

Inside the exceptionally chic guest suite, Luke had practically ripped the dress from her body. Pushing her back against the bed, he'd stared down at her, drinking in the scent of her excitement. The voluptuous view took his breath away, Joanne wearing nothing but her red high-heeled shoes.

Standing above her, he'd stripped down naked, barely pausing to unbutton buttons to get out of the monkey suit that was keeping his flesh from hers. Joanne had gasped with ardent appreciation at the sight of him.

Kneeling before her, Luke had tried desperately to maintain control, but he couldn't hold back. He had to taste her again, wanting to savor the incredible treat that seemed to be teasing him. His mouth enveloped most of the treasure as he sucked her in. Joanne felt a wave of heat like nothing she could ever imagine race from her crotch to deluge her brain. When Luke's tongue swirled around her rigid love button, a wave of heat exploded in her head, and her hips shot up toward the source of all that pleasure.

She'd chanted his name over and over, the mantra fueling his ministrations. "Luke...Luke..." she'd murmured, squirming beneath his hold.

Luke's tongue pushed deeper into her, lapping and licking at the wetness that flowed from her fountain. Joanne cried out again, pushing herself even harder against his face as she succumbed to the desire. As his tongue lashed back and forth over her steaming sex, she couldn't take anymore. She was desperate for the sweet culmination of his loving.

The back of Joanne's head dug deep into the pillows as she arched her spine. For a brief moment she thought of pulling away, but Luke grabbed her thighs and held her still, his eager mouth never losing connection with her body. Joanne's thighs clamped tightly to the sides of the man's head as she rode the waves of sheer delight that had consumed her.

"Don't...stop...I'm..." Joanne had screamed, her body

quivering with the wrenching convulsions of an extreme orgasm. Her pelvis shuddered as she arched her back again. Her mind seemed to explode, as well. As she bucked against the mattress, Luke held her firmly, feeling her writhing and twisting against the sheets. Then as her orgasm had slowly begun to die away, he pulled himself from between her thighs.

Her eyes glazed, her heart thudding in her chest, Joanne reached her arms out to him, wanting to feel him next to her. Moving above her, Luke eased his body gently over hers, allowing his flesh to slowly kiss her flesh—thigh to thigh, belly to belly, torso to torso. He began to kiss her, his lips caressing her lips, her neck, her shoulders, her face, inserting his tongue into her mouth.

Luke didn't think it possible for it to get any hotter, but it did, desire rising with a vengeance to sweep between them. She had slumped into soft compliance beneath him. The familiar ache between his legs raged with fury, desperate to possess her. Sensing his need, Joanne had reached between them to pull pulsating steel into her hand, wrapping her fingers tightly around his manhood.

Luke had inhaled swiftly, leaning his head into her neck as he'd relished the sensations sweeping from his groin. When it had become too much to bear, he'd grabbed her wrist to stall the rhythm of her strokes. "I want to be inside you," he'd whispered softly, reaching for the condom he'd pulled from his wallet. "I want to feel you wrapped around me."

Joanne had looked as if she were holding her breath in anticipation as she'd watched him sheathe his manhood. The engorged protrusion seemed to be moving with a mind of its own as it reached for its target. Gliding her body against him, her pelvis had rotated with want against an erection that had risen full and hungry for her.

His gaze moved up the length of her body until he was staring deep into her eyes. Tears misted his dark orbs, a wealth of emotion gleaming down at her. She had pressed a palm to the side of his face, lifting herself up just enough to meet his mouth with her own.

They held the kiss for just a brief moment, but the connection was the sweetest thing either of them had ever experienced. And then his body had melded with hers, Luke easing himself inside her as he pulled her legs up and around his back.

As they moved in perfect sync, time stood still. Luke pushed and pulled himself from her, his steady plunges pushing them both nearer and nearer to an abyss that they had never known possible. The feeling was too much, moving her own tears to spill past her lashes and dance against her full cheeks. As they'd ridden the last waves of their orgasm together, Luke had held her close, holding her tightly in his arms, vowing to never let the woman go.

Luke took a deep breath as he palmed his crotch with a heavy touch. Just thinking about the woman had him hard all over again, a raging erection pulling tight in his jeans. But something else was weighing down on him, as well. Something he had never experienced before. Whatever it was had a tight grip on his heart. There was no denying that Joanne Lake had him totally and completely spellbound.

Chapter 14

Her laughter was music to his ears, as Luke laughed with her. Joanne was doubled over, salty tears puddled at the edge of her eyes as she neared the point of crying from laughing so hard. Luke shook his head in amusement.

"It really wasn't that funny." He chuckled as they stood in the storage room of the community center, taking an inventory of the supplies.

Joanne nodded her head. "Yes…yes, it was," she gasped, trying to catch her breath. "You should have…should have seen your expression!"

Luke knew the moment had been funny. His brothers were still teasing him about it. He imagined it would take some time to live that moment down. Joanne had joined him at the rodeo, the duo having a grand time watching the many events that had pitted horses and their riders against each other. Trying to show off, Luke had jumped into one of the paddocks, determined to give Joanne a display of his horsemanship. The horse he'd chosen to ride, though, wasn't having any part of Luke's plans. As Luke had tried to settle himself atop the massive animal, the horse had reared down on his front haunches, tossing Luke to the ground.

Luke had looked completely befuddled as he was suddenly sitting butt deep in a pile of horse manure, the horse turning an about-face and swiping the man with a wave of his tail as he eased himself over to the other side of the enclosure. The impression Luke had made was hardly the one he'd hoped for.

"Okay, so maybe it was a little funny," Luke admitted.

Joanne swiped at her eyes with the back of her hand. She took a deep breath of air, filling her lungs, and then a second, blowing warm breath past her lips. "At least you weren't hurt," she said finally. "I wouldn't do that again if I were you."

Luke chuckled. "Not to worry, baby. Matthew can keep his horses."

"Your family was very sweet. I really had a good time."

"I'm glad, Joanne. I had a great time, too." Taking a glance over his shoulder to ensure no one could see them, he leaned to press a light kiss to her lips. "A very nice time," he whispered seductively.

Joanne could feel her cheeks warming, a faint blush washing over her face.

The two had spent most of their time together over the weekend talking. Joanne had wanted to ensure that Luke didn't think she just randomly jumped into bed with every man who showed her an ounce of attention. It had been important to her that Luke understand that the time they'd shared had been exceptionally special, that her attraction to him had not only taken her by surprise but had her feeling something she had never ever felt before for a man. She'd been relieved when Luke had admitted that he was feeling it, as well, wanting her like he'd never wanted any other woman before.

His teasing only served to remind her that she had thrown caution right out the door, engaging in activity, and in places, she had no business. She could feel a full grin pulling at her mouth. Shaking her head, Joanne couldn't begin to explain what had gotten into her. Luke, however, hadn't been at all dismayed by what they had done and where they had done it.

As if he could read her mind, the man pressed another kiss to the back of her neck, allowing his lips to linger there longer than necessary.

"We could lock the door," he whispered, warm breath teasing her earlobe.

"No, we can't." Joanne giggled, turning to face him as she met his mouth in a quick kiss. "Don't even think about it."

Luke laughed. "Oh, I can think about it. That's half the fun."

"Luke Stallion, you are trouble. I can see that now," she said, gliding her index finger along the line of his profile.

He smiled. "Yes, I am," he said, winking. "Think you can handle me?"

"The question, sir, is can you handle me?" she said, her demure tone causing a ripple of heat to pierce his insides.

The man's eyes widened, a full grin spreading across his face. "Oh, baby, that sounds like a challenge."

Joanne laughed warmly, moving out the large door. "Something tells me you'll have no problems with being up for any task, Mr. Stallion. No problems at all."

"I'm up, all right," Luke chimed, following behind her. "Girl, I'm definitely up!"

Time flew. It had taken no time at all before Luke and Joanne had established a comfortable routine with each other. Joanne couldn't begin to imagine herself going back to how it was before Luke had come into her life. She relished the time they spent each evening sharing what each had accomplished during the day.

She was moved by Luke's dedication to the rejuvenation project. His commitment to the community was inspiring, the man moved to restore the area to its original glory. He frequently sought out her opinion, and Joanne was flattered that he respected what she thought and believed in. His interest in her business was encouraging her as well, as Luke pushed her to think outside of the box, allowing her to bounce her ideas off him as he fueled her creativity with his own.

The two were having such a good time together that Joanne hadn't given a second thought to telling him about her father or her history, and Luke hadn't pushed for information that he saw that she was uncomfortable sharing.

Luke understood that there were things in Joanne's life that hadn't always brought her joy. Every so often a look of dismay and hurt would cross her face when he'd ask about her family and her friends. So Luke vowed that if he could avoid it, he would never say or do anything to put that pain in her eyes.

Both were enjoying how their new relationship was developing. Both were awed by their new couple status, never having fathomed that being one half of a whole could have happened so quickly.

The two were seated on the oversized sofa in Luke's

bedroom, a raging fire burning in the fireplace. The day had been long and strenuous and Luke was glad to finally be finished with it. He was also glad that Joanne was there with him, listening to his concerns and readily offering him words of encouragement and advice.

He looked up from the laptop resting on his thighs to stare at her as she pored over dress designs on the other end of the couch. They sat facing each other, their legs entangled across the length of the upholstered cushions. Watching her had become habitual, with Luke stealing glances every opportunity he could. He loved watching her from a distance. Loved how her brow furrowed in concentration when something was challenging her. He adored how her eyes lit up when she was happy, the wealth of it shimmering across her face. Luke found himself reveling in the feeling of deep contentment he was feeling whenever he was with Joanne. Loved feeling like he would be happy to spend the rest of his life lying right there near her. Luke suddenly saw himself holding tight to that feeling forever, never wanting it to end.

He closed his eyes, taking delight in how she caressed the length of his leg with her bare foot. Her touch had provoked every nerve ending in his body to fire with anticipation. Easing his computer to the floor, he leaned back against the armrest, falling into a feel-good moment that had captured his full attention. From the other end of the sofa, Joanne was watching him as intently, her own desire igniting like a brush fire out of control. A sly smile pulled at the corners of her mouth as she drew a heated path from the cusp of his groin down to his ankles.

"Girl, what are you doing to me?" Luke suddenly asked, his voice dropping to a loud whisper. He opened his eyes, staring at her keenly with a look of sheer lust.

Joanne giggled, her manicured toes grazing the wealth

of an erection that was pressing heavily against the confinement of his sweatpants. "Want me to stop?" she asked, as she stroked him with the ball of her foot.

Luke shook his head, leaning his head back against the sofa as he closed his eyes. What she was doing was feeling much too good for him to stop her. Luke didn't notice when Joanne reached for her glass of iced tea on the end table.

A sly smile spread across Joanne's face. Reaching into the liquid, she pulled out a single ice cube. Pulling it to her mouth, she kissed it, sucking it in slowly as she adjusted to the freezing texture against her lips.

Moving up the length of his body, Joanne slowly pushed her hands beneath his T-shirt, moving the fabric to expose his naked skin. Sucking the ice cube into her mouth, Joanne leaned to kiss Luke's bare nipple, allowing the frozen water to snake past her lips and graze his erect nipple. The sudden chill moved Luke to sit upright, wincing ever so slightly. Joanne's gaze met his stare, her palm pushing him back down as she moved to his other nipple, encircling the dark bud with her cold lips. She felt his body jump, his erection pulsing against her abdomen.

Luke clasped his hands together above his head, fighting the urge to push her from him, relishing the intense sensations of hot and cold that were sweeping through his body. His legs shifted against the sofa as he moved to wrap them around the back of her thighs.

Joanne continued to trail a hot-and-cold path down his torso, pausing to sink her tongue into his belly button. Ice water dripped from her mouth and she lapped at it with her tongue. The melting ice caused droplets of water to dribble across the taut muscles of his abdomen, down to the tight curls that peeked from the waistband of his sweats. Luke's head bent backward as he felt a shock of pleasure burn through him. He felt himself stiffen even more, his flesh harder than concrete.

Clasping him around his hips, Joanne pushed at his pants, moving him to lift his hips as she drew the garment over his buttocks. With freedom gained, his erection strained and bobbed with his runaway pulse, begging for attention. When Joanne took him in her mouth, his brain went numb, all coherent thought lost to him.

The sensations were overwhelming, pleasure beyond his comprehension. Joanne rotated her head when he bottomed out in her throat, his engorged member filling her mouth. Luke gasped at the woman's aggressiveness. Joanne had attacked his manhood as if it were necessary for their survival, her ministrations urgent. Luke didn't know how he would be able to last under such an onslaught, his whole body starting to tremble and quake. Every muscle in his body suddenly tensed as Joanne pleasured him like he'd not been pleasured before. His heart was beating heavily in his chest and then his whole body exploded, every one of his senses leaving him a second away from unconsciousness.

As Joanne sat back against the sofa, her gaze still locked on his face, Luke fought to regain his composure. His breathing was erratic, sweat beading across his brow. He opened his eyes and met her stare. Joanne's smile filled him.

"You are staying the night, right?" he finally managed to ask, still gasping for air.

Joanne laughed, tossing her head back against her neck. "Should I stay?"

Luke nodded. "I wouldn't have it any other way."

The smell of coffee invaded Joanne's consciousness. For a brief moment, she wondered where the decadent scent was coming from, and then she remembered the personal coffeepot Luke had set on a timer the evening before.

Sleep had come in the early hours of the morning, their late-night antics keeping them up well past their usual bed times. Luke's naked body was curved warmly around her own nakedness, and Joanne had no desire to rise from where they lay. Luke's breathing was still deep and heavy, and Joanne knew that he was as reluctant to pull himself from the throes of sleep as she was. She heaved a deep sigh.

The man had become a sweet addiction, a craving that she couldn't seem to get enough of, and Joanne was completely enamored with him. Luke Stallion had unleashed a wealth of emotion that Joanne hadn't known she possessed. She felt a sense of freedom with the man, all her inhibitions melting away when they were together. Joanne couldn't begin to fathom the effect he'd managed to have on her usually reserved and conservative personality traits. But Luke had set her inner tiger free, and Joanne had no desire to cage that beast.

She rolled her body against the padded mattress, turning until she was facing the man. She pressed her face into his chest, inhaling the scent of him. Without opening his eyes, Luke wrapped his arms tightly around her torso, hugging her close. His touch was easy and gentle as he slowly caressed her back and shoulders. Joanne snuggled down into the warmth of it.

Whatever was happening between them had taken on a life of its own. Joanne didn't have the words to define what she was feeling for Luke, but she knew that whatever fate might have in store for them, she could easily stay lost in that Stallion's arms forever.

Chapter 15

John and Matthew stood at the back of the oversize conference room, arms folded over their chests as Luke and the team he'd pulled together presented the final details of the rejuvenation proposal.

When every aspect of the project had been explained, analyzed and critiqued, Luke shut off the overhead projector and closed his laptop. Silence filled the space as everyone waited for the senior partners to react. Luke held his breath in anticipation.

Matthew cut an eye at John as he moved to the front of the room. "How soon before you'll be ready to initiate stage one?" Matthew asked, meeting Luke's stare as he sat down.

"All the permit applications can be filed today. I have assurances from the zoning department and the permit office that they'll have them completed within two weeks. There are contracts on the table already for us to officially purchase the necessary property, and we can close in forty-five days. The rest is gravy. All we need is the go-ahead."

Luke looked from Matthew to John, his expression hopeful. He knew he'd done a good job, exceeding everyone's expectations, but he was anxious to hear John say so. He was eager for his older brother to give him the okay to proceed.

John said nothing, a pensive stare focused intently on the younger man. A slow smile finally pulled at John's mouth, lifting it easily. He nodded his head as he strode slowly to the head of the oversized conference table, moving to stand in front of Luke. The two men eyed each other briefly, then John extended his hand, the two men shaking.

"Congratulations, Mr. Vice President. I'll expect a complete progress report every thirty days."

Luke tipped his head in acknowledgment, a wide grin filling his face. "Not a problem."

John lifted his leather portfolio from the table. Moving toward the door, he turned back to the group assembled. "Let's get to work, people. You all have a neighborhood to rebuild."

The three men were like proud fathers celebrating a son's greatest accomplishments. Luke had lost count of the number of times they'd slapped him on the back with joy. Each look of pride bolstered what Luke had known all along. He was ready and capable of doing good things in the world.

He lifted his glass of champagne in another toast, Dom Perignon flowing with ease. "To the rejuvenation project," he chimed cheerily.

His brothers lifted their glasses in response. "To you, little brother," Mark chimed. "A job well done."

"And much success," John added. "We're very proud of you, Luke."

"Thank you."

"So, what's on your agenda tonight?" Mark asked, leaning back in his seat. "Are you planning to celebrate your promotion by doing something special?"

"I think Joanne and I are just going to go to dinner," Luke answered.

"Jo-anne!" Mark said teasingly, emphasizing the syllables in her name. "You and *Jo-anne* have been spending a whole lot of time together lately."

Luke shrugged, a goofy expression painting his face. "Not really."

"Really," Mark said. He looked toward Matthew and John. "The woman is at the house every night *and* every morning!"

"Don't hate," Matthew laughed. "What happened? Now that you're this responsible husband and soon-to-be father, you forget what it's like to be young and carefree?"

John laughed. "Oh, he hasn't forgotten. He just never thought our baby brother would ever be getting more loving than *he's* ever gotten."

Mark waved him off. "I still hold the record, thank you very much."

The brothers all laughed warmly together.

"So," John said, spinning around in his executive's chair. "Are you and Joanne getting serious?"

Luke smiled. "We're enjoying each other. Neither one of us is interested in rushing into anything."

"That's a good thing," Matthew responded. "Don't be like these two. Take your time with it. If she loves you, she's not going anywhere."

Mark cut an eye toward John. Both men grinned widely.

John shook his head. "And if you love her…well…" he paused, his broad shoulders shrugging.

"Do what any good Stallion man would do. Don't let her get away," Mark finished for him.

John lifted his champagne glass. "Preach, my brother!"

The Peony Gardens was a cute little Asian bistro that Luke had insisted she meet him at for dinner. He'd promised a surprise, and the excitement in his voice had been palpable. Joanne had arrived early and was seated at a table that was said to be Mr. Stallion's favorite. Glancing around the room, Joanne could easily see why. From where she sat she had a marvelous view of the water fountains that trickled softly over slate and sandstone. A saltwater fish tank filled an entire wall. Joanne marveled at the brightly colored aquatic life that seemed oblivious to their stares. As soft music billowed from perfectly placed speakers, Joanne could easily understand what Luke found so appealing about the place. The décor was ultra serene and comfortable.

She heard her name being called from across the crowded room. Recognizing the shrill tone, Joanne suddenly wished she could crawl right under a table and disappear. Unfortunately, there would be no avoiding the prim and proper Mrs. Preston Ragsdale III.

"Joanne? Joanne Lake! How are you, darling?" the woman droned, saddling up to where Joanne was seated. The robust woman leaned to air-kiss both of Joanne's cheeks.

Joanne forced a polite smile on her face, glancing over the older woman's shoulder to the restaurant's front door. "Mrs. Ragsdale, how are you?"

"Just peachy, dear, just peachy! Are you dining alone?"

the woman asked, looking around as if a date might mysteriously appear in the seat across from Joanne.

"No, ma'am. I'm meeting a friend."

The older woman nodded, her eyebrows raising ever so slightly. "We haven't seen you in ages, dear. I was just saying to your father that it's been ages since we last saw you."

Joanne nodded. "I'm sure my father told you that business has been keeping me quite busy."

"Charles was saying you're toying with some design thing for us big girls." The woman chuckled as if there was something humorous about that fact.

Joanne could feel her mouth threatening to pull into a dark frown as Mrs. Ragsdale continued.

"I told Charles to just leave you be. My daughter tried her hand at all sorts of frivolous activities before she finally settled down and married. And that center? Are you still volunteering all your time down there?"

"Yes, ma'am."

"That's so admirable. But you're not going to find a husband down there, Joanne."

"I wasn't really looking for a husband, Mrs. Ragsdale. I just enjoy serving the community."

"Huh," the woman grunted, as if the thought of helping someone other than herself was difficult to comprehend. "I keep saying I need to make a donation of some kind. Donations are tax deductible, aren't they?"

Joanne fought to keep the annoyance from showing on her face. She quickly changed the subject. "How is Danielle?" she asked politely.

"She's doing quite well. She married Harold Rollins you know," the woman said, pausing to take a deep breath. "The senator from Maryland," she added, when Joanne's expression failed to register her son-in-law's name. "And they're expecting any day now," she added for good measure."

"How exciting," Joanne exclaimed. She stole a second glance toward the door. To her dismay, Luke was stepping over the threshold. Joanne could feel her stomach tighten into a knot.

"Well, it was very nice to see you again, Mrs. Ragsdale," Joanne added quickly, reaching up from her seat to air-kiss the woman back. "I'd love to do lunch with you and Danielle after she has her baby."

"That would be very nice. I'll definitely call you," Mrs. Ragsdale was saying just as Luke reached the table.

"Mrs. Ragsdale, what a surprise," Luke gushed politely, greeting the matriarch warmly.

"Luke Stallion! Imagine running into you. What brings you to this side of town?"

Luke leaned down to kiss Joanne's lips. "Hey, you," he whispered softly before lifting himself back up. "Just meeting my favorite girl for dinner," he said aloud.

Mrs. Ragsdale looked clearly amused. "My, my, my, Joanne. I was worrying about you finding a husband, and here you are keeping company with one of our more eligible young men. This one comes from some fine Texas stock," she teased, reaching to brush a palm across Luke's cheek. "Some very fine stock, indeed!"

Luke laughed. "Do you two know each other?"

The woman looked from him to her and back again. "Oh, my, yes. I've know Joanne since—"

"Forever!" Joanne interrupted, her voice rising slightly. A nervous giggle bubbled past her lips. "Well, I'll keep an eye out for that donation, Mrs. Ragsdale. And yes, they're all tax deductible."

"Then the check is in the mail," the woman answered, nodding her head enthusiastically. "Well, you two young people enjoy your meal. The sushi is absolutely divine. Make sure you try the sashimi appetizer. It's a wonderful display of tuna and salmon."

"We'll do that," Joanne said, waving goodbye. "And thank you!"

As the woman walked away, Luke couldn't help but notice the blanket of relief that seemed to wash over Joanne's spirit. Her expression was amusing as she tried to not let the emotion show.

"Mrs. Ragsdale is quite the character. Where do you two know each other from?" Luke asked curiously.

Joanne smiled a weak smile. Lifting her glass of iced water from the table, she sipped it slowly before answering. "The community center," she answered, a little white lie slipping off her tongue.

Luke nodded his head. "Her husband and my brother John have had some business dealings."

"So, how was your day?" Joanne asked, wanting to move the conversation as far from the subject of the Ragsdale family as she could. "What was your exciting news?"

Luke grinned, his broad chest seeming to widen where he sat. "You are looking at the newest vice president of Stallion Enterprises. I'll be overseeing the rejuvenation project as well as establishing a whole division dedicated to community restructuring and development."

Joanne's face beamed with pride. "Oh, sweetie, that's wonderful!" she exclaimed, jumping from her seat to wrap her arms around his thick neck. "That's so exciting!"

Luke hugged her warmly, enjoying the feel of having the woman in his arms. He returned the kiss she planted on his mouth, allowing his lips to linger against the warmth of hers. Joanne settled herself down beside him, snuggling beneath the weight of the arm he wrapped around her.

The moment was interrupted by the petite Asian

woman who arrived to take their order. "Mr. Stallion, would you and your guest like to start with drinks and an appetizer?"

"I'd love a cup of green tea," Joanne said, looking toward Luke for assistance. "But you order the food."

Luke chuckled warmly, placing an order for selections of raw fish with rice-and-veggie combinations.

As the waitress walked away, promising to return quickly, Joanne shook her head. "As you can probably tell by the width of my rear end, I'm more of a meat-and-potatoes kind of girl."

Luke ran a warm palm over her thigh, the heat from his fingers tickling the flesh beneath her linen slacks. "I like your rear end, and I love every one of your curves. If meat and potatoes did that for you, then you can trust I'll be keeping you in full supply whenever you wish. You've been well blessed, my darling!"

Joanne laughed. "On that note, I'm going to excuse myself to the ladies' room. Don't eat all the bait before I get back."

Inside the immaculate chamber, Joanne stared into the mirror. She had to tell Luke the truth, she thought to herself. The deception had clearly gone too far. Nor did it truly make any sense to her. Joanne couldn't begin to imagine Luke not wanting to be with her just because of who her father was. Mrs. Ragsdale had been too close a call, and it was only a matter of time before another one of their mutual acquaintances mentioned that she had a father in Luke's presence.

Joanne splashed her face with cool water. Luke would understand, she mused, pondering the conversation the two would have about her history. She pressed a paper towel against the moisture. Luke wouldn't take offense at her not having opened up her personal life to him so soon. Besides, it wasn't like she actually lied. Joanne hoped Luke would understand. She heaved a deep sigh. She would make him understand, she thought, still staring at herself in the mirror as she navigated that conversation in her mind. Joanne took a deep breath, moving toward the exit. There was no time like the present she thought, before she had a change of mind.

Back at the table, Luke was engaged in conversation on his cell phone. He smiled as she sat down, gesturing with his index finger that he'd be done in a quick minute. When he disconnected the call he looked less than pleased about something.

"Is everything okay?" Joanne asked, concern tinting her tone.

The man nodded. "Just a negotiation snag with one of my contractors. Nothing that can't be fixed."

At that moment the waitress returned with their meal, two exceptionally large platters of well-formed Asian delicacies for them to enjoy. Joanne's eyes widened at the sight. Looking at Luke, she could only shake her head.

The man lifted a shrimp-and-rice combination from the plate with a set of wooden chopsticks, dipping it into a tiny dish of soy sauce. Guiding it toward her mouth, he encouraged her to give the treat a try. "Taste this," Luke said softly. "I promise you'll love it."

Pressing her palm to the back of his hand, Joanne guided it past her lips, chewing it slowly. It tasted better than anticipated, as she savored the delicate combination of flavors. "Not bad, Mr. Stallion, not bad at all," she said.

"I'd never steer you wrong, Ms. Lake. Never."

Joanne was suddenly moved by Luke's brilliant smile. She adjusted the napkin in her lap, folding it over and over again. "Luke, there's something I need—" she started, just as the cell phone on the table chimed for attention.

"I'm sorry, baby, I really need to take this call," Luke said, flipping the device open. "Luke Stallion."

Joanne heaved a heavy sigh, reaching for another piece of sushi. Maybe the conversation could wait until later, she mused. She nodded her head ever so slightly. Later would probably be better for them both.

Chapter 16

Matthew's stare was locked on John's face. John's gaze was locked on the three well-dressed men exiting the doors of the private, members-only club. The afternoon meeting they'd just completed hadn't gone as well as either would have hoped. Both men gestured for their waiter at the same time.

"Bring us another round," Matthew said to the young man who'd rushed to their side, eager to please them both.

"Yes, sir, Mr. Stallion. Will you gentlemen be staying for dinner this evening?" the young man asked, looking from one to the other.

John met his brother's gaze. "No, thank you, Darryl. I'm headed home to my wife."

"I'm going home to his wife, too," Matthew said with a wry smile.

Darryl looked at him curiously.

"Family dinner," Matthew said, explaining himself.

John shook his head, his gaze moving back to the door, the three well-dressed men no longer in view.

Matthew sensed the thoughts that were racing through his brother's mind. "So, what now?" he questioned.

John's expression was stoic. He met his brother's gaze. "Well, we know which shareholders will support us and which won't. So we do the only thing we can do. Prepare for a proxy fight. Do we know anything about E-Kal yet?"

Matthew shrugged. "We know they're privately owned. We know they sit under the umbrella of two other parent companies, and we know that for some reason someone has gone to some significant lengths to keep their true ownership under wraps. We know as much as any other citizen off the street knows."

"And we have no other leads?"

Matthew smiled, lifting a freshly filled glass of bourbon to his lips. "I didn't say that."

John chuckled. "And you'll share this wealth of information soon, I hope?"

"Very soon. The private investigator I put on this says they'll have a report to us in another day or so."

John nodded, reaching for his own glass. "Have you talked to Mark today? I left a message that we were going to meet here, but he never returned my call."

"He flew to Chicago to interview a potential driver for the race team. Said that with him and Mitch expecting, he wants to cut back on his driving. Doesn't want to take any unnecessary risks."

"I can appreciate that."

Matthew nodded.

"How are you doing?" John asked, sibling concern filling his spirit. "What's happening with you and Vanessa?"

Matthew chuckled. "You sound like your wife now."

"You two have us curious. All Vanessa talks about is her baby, and you're not talking at all."

The man smirked. "There's really nothing to tell. Vanessa's having a baby, and like the rest of you I will support her in any way I can."

"Is that your way of telling me to stay out of your business?"

"That's my way of ending the conversation because there is nothing to tell." Matthew changed the subject. "How's Luke doing?"

John shifted the topic with him, duly noting Matthew's sudden discomfort. He knew when to push and when not to. He also knew that his brother would share what he wanted, when he wanted. "He's making some impressive strides. At the rate his project is moving, he should finish earlier than projected and well under budget."

"Good business."

"Very good business!" John gestured with his head. "Has he talked to you about him and Joanne?"

Matthew shrugged. "Not really, but he seems serious. He says they're just enjoying each other, but they're worse than you and Marah were. They're spending all their free time together."

John chuckled. "Don't hate. This, too, could be your life."

Matthew laughed with him. "I like my life just fine, thank you very much."

The two men continued to chat comfortably as they savored the last of their cocktails. Their time was interrupted by the waiter and the club's manager rushing to the table. The man extended his hand toward John and then Matthew, shaking theirs eagerly.

"Matthew, I hate to interrupt, but we have a situation."

"What's wrong, Daniel?"

"The police are at the front desk. It would seem that someone stole your Mercedes from the parking lot. There was a chase and it was involved in an accident on I-35."

"Well, I'll be…" Matthew started, the words stalling on his tongue.

John rose from his seat, and Matthew followed suit. "Do you know if anyone was hurt, Daniel?"

"They didn't say, but an officer would like to speak with the owner."

The two men followed on the manager's heels as Darryl brought up the rear behind them. John threw a look over his shoulder, giving his brother a smug smile. "I really liked that car on you, too."

Joanne was curled up on the Brooks family sofa, her head nestled in Mama Estelle's lap. The older woman was gently stroking her brow, clucking softly under her breath. Joanne swiped tears from her eyes with the back of her hand.

"Don't make no kind of sense, Joanne. None whatsoever."

"I know, Mama Estelle. Honest, I've tried to tell Luke a few times, but I can never seem to get the words out. Either we get interrupted or I get cold feet."

"He's not going to be happy about it, by no means, but you can't build a relationship on half-truths, baby. Honesty is the foundation of any successful relationship. And communication is key. You need to do better at both."

"Haven't you ever done something, Mama Estelle, that just snowballed out of control? Because that's what happened here. My intentions were good, but it's just gotten away from me."

The matriarch blew warm breath in a deep sigh. "You're

making excuses for bad behavior. You know better. I taught you better."

Joanne had no response, falling silent as Mama Estelle hummed a soft spiritual in her ear. Joanne knew she should have told Luke by now. She knew that the longer she kept her paternity a secret, the worse it would be when she did tell. Denying the lifestyle she'd been raised in, pretending that Luke's world was as far from her own as she could imagine, wasn't doing either of them an ounce of good. Neither was the secret that had brought her to the only home that had always made her feel safe and secure.

Joanne had woken early, nestled deep against Luke's broad back. Wrapping her arms around his waist, she'd snuggled against his warmth, relishing the tranquility she'd found being by his side.

Rising, the two had showered together, their morning ritual starting her day off nicely. No one had blinked any eye when the two had found their way to the breakfast table, Joanne pulling two ceramic mugs from the cupboards and filling them both with freshly brewed coffee.

She and Michelle had chatted briefly, the two women having formed a nice friendship since Joanne had begun to spend so much of her time in the Stallion home. Michelle's excitement over her pregnancy had been infectious, and it moved Joanne to fantasize such an event for herself. Even Mark had teased her and Luke about legitimizing their relationship so that the impending addition to their family might have a cousin or two to grow up with. Luke had laughed it off, but even he had to admit to himself that the thought of fathering a child with Joanne piqued his interest.

Then Mark had opened the morning newspaper, the daily headline in the business section capturing his full attention. The print was bold, jumping off the page as if it were being shouted over an intercom. E-Kal Makes Bid For Stallion Empire. As he'd read the details out loud, Joanne had felt her stomach rise into her throat, threatening to spew her breakfast before it could settle. She was shocked, the emotion dressing her expression. She couldn't begin to believe this was happening to her.

Both brothers had clearly been chagrined by the whole affair. Joanne had been mortified to learn that the Stallion nemesis was the one and only Charles Lake. Both Luke and his brother had soon raced from their family's home, knowing that their whole day would be occupied with the fallout from the news.

Umpteen messages to her father had gone unanswered, the man tied up in corporate meetings for most of the day. But Joanne was desperate to speak to him. Desperate to make this whole mess go away. Unable to focus, she'd finally found her way to Estelle Brooks's front door, doing what she did best when she needed her father—waiting patiently for the man to show her an ounce of his attention.

Joanne didn't know how long she'd been sleeping, but she was startled awake by the easy chime of her cell phone. Marley and her mother were nowhere to be found. The home was dark and quiet as she fumbled for her purse, searching anxiously for the ringing device. Pulling it into her hand, she glanced quickly at the caller ID before answering it.

"Daddy! I've been calling you all day."

"I'm a busy man, Joanne. What's the problem?"

"You're trying to steal Stallion Enterprises. That's what the problem is."

"I'm not trying to steal anything, Joanne. I've offered to pay them fair market value for their business."

"Obviously the Stallion family wasn't interested in your offer."

"Obviously, but as one of their major stockholders, I believe our company will be better suited to run that business."

"*Our* company? There is no *our* in this, Daddy. That company and this decision is yours, and yours alone."

"That's where you're wrong, Joanne. E-Kal is very much *our* company. I built that business for you. It's your legacy. One day I'll pass the reins over to you and you'll pass them down to your own children. Right now I have to do everything I can to ensure that it's worth inheriting."

"Why Stallion Enterprises, Daddy? Why, out of all the companies you could have purchased, why did you choose Stallion?"

"It's a strategic move, Joanne. Stallion Enterprises is exceptionally profitable. They have great distribution capabilities in areas we need to be in. If we acquire Stallion, then it allows us to enter new markets without having to take on the risk, time and expense of starting new divisions. Why wouldn't I want them?"

"Don't do this, Daddy. I've never asked you for anything before, but I'm asking you to not to do this. Leave the Stallions alone. Go after someone else's company. Please."

"Don't be ridiculous, Joanne. It's not like you know the Stallions. What difference does it make?"

"It makes a difference to me. Please, Daddy!" Joanne pleaded.

Her father laughed, and Joanne could almost see him shaking his head as if she'd asked him for the moon. How absurd of her to think that he might actually make an effort to attain the moon for her. How foolish was she to think that he might actually do something for his daughter that she actually wanted him to do.

Charles Lake dismissed her and her wants. "Daughter, you go dabble with your little design thing and let me deal with the real business. My attorney will be sending some papers over for your signature this week. Sign them and give them right back to the messenger. Understand?"

Joanne didn't bother to respond. Without another word, she disconnected the call. Across the room, the digital clock on the bookcase glimmered the time in florescent green. It was barely eight o'clock in the evening.

Flipping the phone open a second time, she pressed the speed-dial number for Luke. He answered on the first ring.

"Hey, buddy!"

"Hey, yourself. How are you?"

"Exhausted. I've had some kind of day. How are you doing?"

"I've been better. I've had a day, too."

"Where are you?" Luke asked.

Joanne looked around the quaint room, family photographs of Mama Estelle, Marley and the rest of the Brooks clan seeming to stare back at her. "I'm home," she said finally, tears pressing hot against her closed eyelids.

"Have you had dinner yet?" Luke queried. His voice dropped to a soft whisper. "I really would like to see you. I really *need* to see you, Joanne."

Joanne shook her head into the receiver as if he could see her. "No, but I don't have much of an appetite. I just want you to hold me," she said, whispering back.

Something in her voice pulled at Luke's heartstrings. "Is everything okay, baby?"

Gently shaking her head, Joanne fought back the urge to cry. "I'm fine. I just miss you."

A pregnant pause filled the space over the telephone line. It swelled full, looming like an elephant in a small room. Both of them sensed the other wanting to say something, but neither one could find the words. Luke finally broke the silence.

"The house has been turned into battle-zone central. Everyone's here, and it doesn't look like they're going anywhere anytime soon. Why don't you meet me at the Ritz-Carlton?"

"I'm leaving now," Joanne said, nodding.

As Joanne disconnected the call, she dropped the phone to the floor and her head into her hands. She had to tell Luke about her connection to E-Kal. He had to hear it from her before he heard it from someone else. But she would have given anything to make it all go away so that Luke would never have to hear a thing.

Chapter 17

His kisses were precious, like exquisite gems to be marveled over. Since coming through the penthouse doors Joanne had been standing in Luke's arms for a full ten minutes, his mouth gently caressing her own. Joanne melted beneath his touch, his large hands stroking every ounce of worry from the length of her arms, her back, the curve of her hips and her waist. Joanne willed the moment to last forever.

Leaning her head back against her shoulders, Joanne swallowed hard as Luke's kisses moved down the length of her neck and back again. His heated breath generated an explosion of sensation that threatened to rob her of her consciousness. Her legs quivered uncontrollably, threatening to drop her to the ground.

Joanne leaned her head into Luke's chest, wrapping her arms around his midsection. Her grip was telling, the woman holding on to Luke for dear life. So Luke held her, wrapping his arms tightly around her shoulders and hugging her to him. He held her close as he gently rocked her in his arms, leaning his cheek next to hers.

They needed to talk, but Joanne couldn't find the words to say what she needed to say to him. Any attempt at rational thought disappeared in the whirlwind of emotions. Luke had resumed his trail of kisses, his tongue grazing her lips in sweet invitation. Joanne closed her eyes, tilted her head back to meet his mouth and allowed herself to fall into the emotion. Her lips parted, and Luke's tongue slipped softly between them.

The kiss was heated, rising in urgency, and then Luke broke the sweet connection, his mouth fluttering across her cheeks, her nose and her eyelids before tracing a second path past the sensitive lobe of her ear, across her jawline, back down her neck to the hollow between her collarbone. Joanne gasped softly for air.

"How's your day now?" Luke whispered into her ear, nuzzling his face against her neck.

Joanne murmured softly, "It's much better now."

"So is mine, now that I'm with you." Luke's smile was tender, and Joanne felt herself lost in the beauty of it. He clasped her hands in his and pulled her gently into the immaculately decorated room. Guiding her to the upholstered sofa that adorned one side of the luxury suite, the two settled down against the cushions.

Luke pulled Joanne back against his chest, wrapping the length of his arms around her torso. He gently caressed her arms, his fingers kneading the tension from her body. Luke nuzzled his face into her hair, inhaling deeply. The soft strands smelled of coconut and almonds.

Soft music filled the space. The tune playing was familiar, but Joanne couldn't attach a name or performer to it. She closed her eyes, allowing the subtle lilt of flutes and violins to flood her senses, Luke's soft touch leading the intimate moment.

"This is nice," she finally whispered, breaking the silence that had risen between them. "I wish we could stay like this forever."

The man nodded his agreement. "So do I."

Joanne turned in her seat to face him. "Luke, there is so much I need to tell you. There are things you need to know about me and—"

"Wait," Luke whispered, cutting her off. He clasped her face between his large hands, pressing his fingers to her furrowed brow.

Joanne could feel herself becoming lost in the deep stare that he gave her, the dark pools pulling her in. "But, I have to tell you—"

"Baby, I want to know everything there is to know about you," he said, shaking his head. "You know I do. But tonight I just want us to enjoy the moment. This whole day has been one nightmare after another. I just want to spend the rest of the night holding you in my arms and making love to you. Tomorrow, when we wake up, we can talk about everything or nothing, whatever you want. Okay? Please?"

Joanne felt her head bobbing against her neck. She met his smile with one of her own and then he kissed her again, embracing her tightly. Luke snuggled his face into Joanne's neck, the fruity scent of her body wash tickling his nostrils. He could almost taste the light mango scent against her smooth, chocolate body. Unable to resist, Luke planted gentle kisses on her soft neck, his tongue flickering against the soft curve beneath her chin. Joanne groaned as a current of electricity sped through her body, shivers of energy coursing through her veins.

Joanne traced her index finger along the line of his

profile. The slim appendage drew a delicate trail over the chiseled cheekbones down to his full lips. Luke opened his mouth and captured the firm digit between his teeth. Luke sucked softly on the sweet flesh, drawing it in and out. As Luke sucked harder, Joanne's passion rose tenfold, warm waves of pleasure rushing through her.

Sliding her finger from his mouth, Luke pressed a warm kiss to the palm of her hand. Unable to resist, Joanne leaned in and pressed her lips against his. Luke moaned as Joanne's soft tongue entered his mouth, softly caressing his own. Their kisses deepened as Luke gripped the back of Joanne's head and locked his fingers in her soft, silky curls. Desire nourished desire, a deep hunger consuming them both as they danced back and forth in each other's mouths.

A flash of heat burned deep between Joanne's thighs. Lifting her body above his, she pushed him gently back against the cushions. Straddling his body, she parted her legs widely around his pelvis, grinding herself against him. A full erection strained hard and urgent in response.

The dance against him was slow and methodic, and Joanne savored the sensations. She understood that tomorrow and all their secrets would come soon enough, but this night would be theirs alone. All she wanted was to make love to him and have their lovemaking last a lifetime.

As if reading her mind, Luke grabbed her buttocks with both hands, pulling her tight to him as he rotated his body in sync with hers. His flesh was rigid, a rod of steel desperate to be free as Joanne rode him through his clothes.

Joanne's skin felt like it was on fire, and she no longer had any control over her muscles. Their lips found each other again, and the kiss deepened as she felt Luke's hands disappearing beneath her T-shirt. He fumbled briefly, unclasping her bra. The sudden release of her breasts swinging to freedom emboldened him, and he quickly cupped each mound in his palms. His fingers slid over the sensitive nipples, which reacted to his touch as he caressed the swollen orbs.

Luke finally broke the kiss between them. The disconnect left Joanne hungry, and she lifted her questioning eyes to his. Joanne gasped loudly as Luke suddenly lifted himself from the seat, lifting Joanne with him. He held her firmly, her legs wrapping around his waist. His chuckle was teasing as she held on tightly, clasping her hands behind his neck.

Carrying her to the bed, Luke laid her gently against the mattress, snatching the bed covering to the floor. The couple was suddenly fraught with a sense of urgency. Joanne lifted her torso slightly, pulling her shirt and bra up and over her head. She tugged at the button that secured her jeans, sliding her hips from them as she dropped her garments over the side of the bed.

Luke watched, his dark gaze locked with hers as he stepped out of his own clothes, throwing them to the floor with hers. Dropping his naked body down beside hers, Luke pulled Joanne's arms up and over her head, clasping her wrists in his large hand. He stared down at her, enamored with the sheer beauty of her.

"I love you," Luke whispered loudly, his seductive voice coming deep and husky in his throat.

Joanne's eyes widened, but before she could respond, Luke leaned and kissed her deeply. When his mouth met hers in a heated kiss, all thought was lost to them both.

Blanketing her body with his own, Luke savored the sensation—thigh to thigh, belly button to belly button, and lip to lip. Time stopped as they shared space and air, playing each other like skilled musicians would play fine instruments. The simpatico was a sweet, tender melody, and Luke became their conductor.

Joanne lost herself completely as she gave into the sensations Luke was eliciting from her body. When he sheathed himself with a condom, her mind and body were mush. Her back arched and her breathing became labored.

Luke stared down at her, awed by just how beautiful she was. Anticipation danced in her eyes as she opened herself to him, spreading her legs open widely as he tap-danced at the entrance of her private door. Joanne locked her eyes with his as he rocked his pelvis against hers, and then he entered her.

Joanne cried out with pleasure, her soft moans escaping past her lips. Goose bumps covered her entire body and her senses were on overload. With every stroke a shock of pleasure coursed through her. Joanne's eyes were clenched shut, her head rolling from side to side in pure ecstasy.

Luke felt her muscles tighten around him. The vibrations had him quivering, perspiration beading against his skin. They both moved higher and higher toward ecstasy as Luke stroked deeper and deeper into her. Joanne's shuddering moans incited his own, both of them moved to tears.

Orgasm blended into orgasm. Muscles clenched and released as rainbows of color exploded between them. Shocks of pleasure rolled in upon each other, overlapping and rippling away, only to be overshadowed by more crashing waves.

As the spasms died away, Luke held her tightly. Joanne kissed him softly, her body still entangled with his. Then she whispered his name, the lilt of it sweet music to his ears, as she told him she loved him, too.

* * *

The room filled quickly with morning light, rousing Luke from a deep sleep. All was quiet around them, Joanne dozing soundly by his side. Luke suddenly couldn't imagine himself waking any other way. He turned over on his side to face her, wrapping his arms around her sleeping form. The warmth of her body next to his never ceased to cause a ripple of yearning through his body. Every time they were together he wanted her more, unable to get enough of her. His heartbeat raced, beating like thunder in his chest.

They'd made love most of the night, over and over again. He could still feel the heat of her breath against his flesh as he'd swam in the sweetness of her nectar. His entire body had ached for her as she'd mounted him, agonizing expressions of lust and pleasure washing over them both. Heaven had descended down upon them time and time again. The memory rippled through his heart, surging full force through his veins. Luke inhaled, filling his lungs with a deep breath of morning air.

He let his hands roam casually over her nakedness, appreciating her curvaceous hips and thighs and the round fullness of her rear end. With a feathery touch he traced every soft dip and curve.

Joanne stirred as Luke planted a soft kiss against her shoulder. She purred softly. "Good morning."

"Good morning, love."

"What time is it?"

"Too early, but I have to get back to the house."

Joanne snuggled closer against him. "Do you have to? Can't we just stay here all day?"

Luke chuckled. "That would be nice, but duty calls."

Joanne sighed, wanting to linger in the moment for as long as she could. Being with Luke, secure in his arms, was all she wanted, and the yearning was like nothing she'd ever experienced before. "We still need to talk," she said.

Luke nodded. "We will. I promise. For now, though, come back to the house with me for breakfast. Then we'll talk tonight over dinner. Okay?"

Joanne paused before nodding her head against his chest. Reaching between them, Joanne wrapped a warm palm around his morning erection. She glanced up to his face. "Do we have time to…" she said, rising lust shimmering in her eyes.

Luke laughed. "I don't see any reason why we can't make time."

She laughed with him. "Mr. Stallion, I do like the way you think."

Chapter 18

Looking around the library of the Preston Hollow home, John was reminded of everything he'd accomplished for his family. Since day one everything he'd done had been for the people he loved. The magnificent estate on Audubon Avenue had eventually become home to him and his brothers. But it had taken some hard times and much hard work to make that happen.

John appraised the room a second time. The handsome study was complemented by Brazilian cherrywood floors, wall-to-wall built-in bookcases and a beamed ceiling. It was one of his favorite rooms in the house. It was the library his mother had dreamed of having for herself.

Flashing back to shortly after the death of their parents, John remembered coming home to a teary-eyed Luke. The eight-year-old had been inconsolable. John had barely made it through the front door before his little brother had glued himself to John's side, sobbing uncontrollably. It had taken seventeen-year-old John a full fifteen minutes to decipher that little Luke was petrified of them not having a home of their own. It had taken another thirty minutes to convince the kid that he would have the best home John could muster.

When all was said and done, the child's smile didn't compare to the grin that had been plastered on his face when three years later John had given him his very own key to Preston Hollow. With some fifteen thousand square feet of living space and acreage that boasted a putting green, an Olympic-size swimming pool and tennis courts, the house had surpassed all of their expectations. Love, trust and respect between the four siblings had made it a home they were each proud of. Although Mark and Luke were the only two still residing there, it was still very much the family home.

Now, he and his brothers were fighting to hold on to everything they'd built. Someone was threatening their security and all four brothers were determined to make sure that didn't happen.

He took a quick glance to the Rolex watch on his wrist. It was minutes away from seven o'clock in the morning. John had fallen asleep in the leather recliner sometime after three o'clock that morning. He and Matthew and their legal team had worked well into the night and early morning to prepare their case against E-Kal. For hours the team had debated strategy. From back-end buyouts to a white-knight defense, they'd argued the pros and cons of every tactic against the hostile takeover they could fathom. No stone had been left unturned as they'd considered every possible scenario and its potential outcome.

John yawned, stretching his body upward. He was just contemplating a hot shower when Mark came into the room, two cups of steaming coffee in his hands.

"Figured you'd be awake by now," Mark said, passing one cup into John's hands.

"Too much work to do, bro. Too much work to do. How are you doing this morning?"

Mark shrugged. "Mitch has morning sickness twenty-four hours a day. She's miserable, so I'm miserable."

John chuckled. "I'm sure it'll get better soon."

Mark laughed with him. "I sure hope so."

The senior Stallion blew a heavy sigh, blowing air over the hot brew. "Have you seen Matthew?"

"He's upstairs taking a shower," Mark said, gesturing with his index finger.

"What about Luke?"

Mark's shoulders pushed skyward. "Who knows. He didn't come back last night. Called to say he was staying with Joanne."

John rolled his eyes to the ceiling. "Young love..."

Both men grinned as they fell into a vat of silence, savoring the comfort of quiet and the rich, robust flavor of their morning beverage. Their night had been long. The day would probably be even longer. This brief respite was a welcome reprieve. Minutes later when the front doorbell rang neither one made any effort to see who was calling or why.

On the second ring they heard Michelle fussing about where everyone was. When Matthew's booming voice and a woman's sharp laughter were stirred into the mix, both men knew their moment of reflection had come to an end. Before either could form a second thought, Vanessa came barreling into the room, Matthew following close on her heels.

"Good morning, Boo!" she said, reaching to kiss John's cheek. She greeted Mark with a hearty embrace. "Hey, Big Daddy!"

Moved by her vitality, both men smiled. "What brings you here so early, Vanessa, or do we need to ask?" Mark said, raising an eyebrow toward Matthew.

Vanessa laughed heartily. Matthew didn't find the comment funny and said so.

"Actually, I'm here on serious business," Vanessa said, reaching into the leather attaché slung over her shoulders. "You all need to see this." She passed a manila folder to John.

"What's this?"

Vanessa glanced toward Mark then back to John. "It's some information your brother wanted me to track down for you. I told y'all before I've got some mad private-eye skills."

Vanessa swung back around to take a seat on the upholstered love seat. "What's for breakfast? I'm hungry!"

The room grew silent as John flipped through the wealth of data that had been collected. The light in his eyes darkened considerably as something caught his attention, moving him to turn his back to the group as he continued to read.

Matthew and Mark both grew concerned as they stood watching. Vanessa's smile was still wide as she nodded. "It's some mess, huh?" Vanessa said, peering toward John.

Glancing over the top of the folder, John cast his eyes down to the woman. "Are you absolutely certain about this, Vanessa?"

She nodded. "Absolutely, positively. I've checked, double-checked and triple-checked all the facts."

John closed the folder, his shoulders slouching as he fell back into the leather recliner. He pulled a fist to his mouth, his eyes closed as he fell into thought.

"What?" Matthew and Mark both asked, sounding like surround sound in the room.

John said nothing, blowing warm breath into the morning air. Extending his hand, he passed the folder to Matthew. Soon his expression matched his brother's. After reading and rereading the information, he passed the folder to Mark.

"Well, I'll be damned..." Mark exclaimed loudly.

Before anyone else could comment, Luke and Joanne slid into the room, hand in hand.

"Hey, good people!" Luke chimed happily.

"Good morning," Joanne echoed.

Everyone in the room turned to stare, their gazes focused on Joanne, each of them appraising her. Joanne stared back, meeting each gaze one by one. The sudden tension in the room was palpable.

Vanessa rose from her seat. "I smell bacon cooking. I'll just leave y'all to it. If you need some backup, me and Mitch will be in the kitchen. Just holla!" she said as she eased toward the door. As she passed by Joanne she shook her head, her expression daunting. "Humph," she muttered loudly. "Humph."

Dread suddenly blanketed Joanne's face, an unsavory feeling rising in the pit of her stomach. She could tell from the stares she was getting that her secret had been exposed. She couldn't believe this was happening to her. Her good morning wasn't feeling quite so good anymore.

"What's going on?" Luke asked. "What's Vanessa's problem? He looked from one brother to another. "Did something happen?"

Rising from his seat, John moved to Mark's side, pulling the manila folder from his hands. He passed the folder to Luke. He met Joanne's gaze briefly before turning to sit back down.

Joanne grabbed Luke's forearm, tightly clutching him. "Luke, baby, I have to tell you something. I'm so sorry..." she gasped, tears rising to her eyes.

Flipping open the folder, Luke quickly scanned its contents. The short period of time felt like an eternity as the young man focused on one piece of data that screamed up at him. Jerking his arm from her touch, Luke moved to his brother's side, turning to stare at the woman. A frown flashed across his face and he swallowed angrily. "Joanne, is this true?"

Joanne's tears rolled over her cheeks. She nodded. Luke's stare had gone cold, the gleam in his eyes harsh. Joanne could feel a rift widening between them. "Luke, I didn't mean for this—" she started.

Luke cut her off, shaking his head. "You played me. I trusted you, and you played me. All this time I thought you cared about me, and you were playing me."

Joanne stepped toward him, clutching the front of Luke's shirt. "I didn't...I wanted to tell you. I tried..."

Clutching her by the shoulders, Luke pushed her from him, the gesture sending her backward into the wall. They locked eyes for just a brief moment, then without saying another word he rushed out of the room, leaving all of them behind.

Their silence had been deafening and expressive. It had been a bleak, brooding silence that seemed to spell out a wealth of anger. Joanne had begged them to understand that she hadn't had anything to do with her father's battle for control of Stallion Enterprises. She tried to explain, and not one of the brothers had had anything to say to her until Matthew had politely asked her to leave their home, gently escorting her by the elbow to the front door. Luke had disappeared from sight, refusing to answer when she'd called for him. The Stallion limo had been dispatched to take her wherever she wanted to be taken, and Joanne had been sobbing ever since.

Marley stared at her from across the room, her head shaking. Her best friend had tried to console her and had failed, unable to find the words to assure Joanne that it would all work itself out. Not even Marley believed Joanne could make this mess well again.

"You love him, don't you?" Marley asked, crossing her arms over her chest.

Joanne lifted her bloodshot eyes to stare at the woman. She nodded her head, her tears beginning to fall once again. "I do. I didn't mean for this to happen, Marley. Now I don't know what to do."

"Give that boy some time," Mama Estelle said from her seat at the kitchen table. "Give him some time and then you need to talk to him. Communication is key," she repeated for the umpteenth time.

Joanne nodded, dropping her head back against the arm of the sofa. She had no doubts that she would have plenty of time before Luke Stallion would want to speak to her about anything ever again.

"She played me! All this time she was only trying to weasel her way inside. I can't believe I fell for it."

"What you fell for was her. Admit it. You've fallen in love with Joanne."

Luke cut his eyes toward Michelle. The woman had a sly smirk on her face. He frowned in response, his lips forming a tight line. He ignored her comment.

"Why'd she do it, Mitch? Why? Why would she lie to me like that?"

"Did she lie? Is that what she did? You said she always

avoided questions about herself. What was it she actually said to you?"

Luke paused for a moment to reflect. When he didn't say anything, Michelle rose from her seat, moving to his side. She wrapped her arms around his shoulders and hugged him tightly. Pressing a kiss to his forehead, she patted him gently against the back.

"Give it some time," Michelle whispered softly. "If it's meant to be it'll work itself out." She moved toward the door. "If you need to talk I'll be at the garage. Just call me," she said as she waved goodbye.

Nodding, Luke knew with a high degree of certainty that he wouldn't be calling. He wasn't much interested in talking about Joanne with anyone.

Luke sat in the home's Victorian conservatory. It was a light-drenched glass chamber that looked out over the landscaped property outside. The morning sky had gone from a brilliant blue to a profusion of blue-gray clouds threatening to explode rain down over the land. The shift in climate mirrored his mood.

Luke lifted his legs onto a chaise, settling back against the plush cushions. He took a deep breath, then two, holding both briefly before blowing the stale air past his full lips.

The folder in his lap felt like a lead weight bearing down against his thighs. It weighed even heavier against his heart. He flipped through the documents again, wading through the details that had connected all the dots.

E-Kal Industries. *Lake* spelled backwards. A privately owned enterprise headed by Joanne's father, Dr. Charles Lake. How could she not have known? She was listed as an active officer of the business! How could Joanne not have told him all of this?

More important to him, though, was understanding how she could have told him she cared about him if she didn't?

Luke tossed the folder and its contents to the floor. Clasping his hands behind his head, he stared skyward. What he really wanted to know was what Joanne Lake truly felt for him, if all the two had shared had only been a lie.

Chapter 19

"I messed up," Luke said to his brothers. He stared from one dark face to another. "I told her everything. I thought she…" The young man hesitated.

"Don't beat yourself up," John said calmly. "I tell Marah everything, too. And I'm sure Mark vents to Mitch after a hard day, as well."

Mark nodded. "That's right. If you can't share your thoughts with your woman, who can you share them with?"

"I trusted her. I can't believe she…"

John cut his eyes at Matthew and Luke. "You need to talk to her," he said firmly.

"No!" Luke shook his head vehemently. "That's not going to happen."

"That's a mature response," Matthew said sarcastically.

Luke shrugged. "Sure, that's easy for you to say. The

woman you love didn't lie to you. Not that I recall you ever being in a situation like this before."

"No, she didn't," Matthew responded. "But if she had we would definitely be having a conversation about it. And watch your tone. You ain't that grown, little brother. I can still whup yo' tail if I have to."

Luke tossed up his hands in frustration.

John shook his head. "Luke, you have to do what you feel is right for you. We can't tell you what that is. But we can tell you from our own experiences what we think is right, not that you have to agree. Bottom line, though, is that not talking to Joanne isn't going to solve a thing between you two. Avoiding her is not going to give you any answers or make the situation different."

John rose from his seat. "On that note, we have a team of attorneys to meet with. They'll need to know exactly what you might have shared with Joanne that can be used against us, if anything at all. For all we know, nothing you shared is important. After that we need to prepare for the shareholders' meeting. We need to do everything we can to ensure that as many votes as possible are in our favor."

"So, does anyone else have anything before we head to the conference room?" John looked from Mark to Matthew to Luke, his gaze lingering on his baby brother's face.

Luke shook his head no.

Matthew cleared his throat, rising from his own seat. "Yeah, I do," he said, turning to their youngest kin. "I will tell you what I told John when he and Marah fell out. If you truly love this woman, then talk to her. You owe yourself that."

It had been two full weeks since Luke had turned his back on her. He wouldn't take her telephone calls, wouldn't answer her messages and he was avoiding every place the two might have run into each other. Joanne got sad and then angry every time she thought about it.

She couldn't believe this was happening to them. If she had just been open about everything from the beginning, things might be different now. She heaved a deep sigh.

Climbing out of her bed, she dragged herself into the bathroom. Staring into the vanity mirror, she cringed. Maybe it was a good thing Luke didn't want to see her, she thought.

I look bad, Joanne mused. Her eyes were bloodshot and her face was blotchy from crying so hard. Her hair was standing on end, and she was certain she'd gained twenty pounds from the steady diet of ice cream and potato chips she'd been soothing her hurt feelings with.

Joanne reached for the shower faucet, turning on the hot water. *This has to end,* she thought. She had to figure out some way to fix this mess. Stripping out of her pajamas, she stepped into the heated moisture. The water felt soothing as it flowed over her face and down the fullness of her body.

Joanne inhaled deeply, wrapping her arms tightly around her body to hug herself. She missed Luke. She missed him so much it actually frightened her. She would never have believed it possible to love a man as much as she found herself loving that man. She loved him, and she wanted him back, and she was willing to do whatever was necessary to make that happen.

Luke slowed his pace down to a moderate jog as he took his eighth lap around the half-mile-long track at the Cooper Aerobics Center. His body hurt, and his muscles were beginning to burn from exhaustion. He'd been pushing his body harder than he needed to, and he was beginning to feel the stress. He knew that it was only a matter of time before the burn would rise to the brink of unbearable and he would want to quit. At some point his body would fail him if he didn't just give in to it.

His thighs and calves had begun to quiver. His heart was starting to beat harshly against the walls of his chest, his lungs crying for a cool breeze of relief. But he refused to stop, adamant that he would not give in to the pain. As long as he ran he wouldn't have to think about Joanne. Joanne, and the hurt in his heart. He refused to let that ache, or his discomfort, consume and control him.

Slowing down even more, his chest heaved up and down as he began to walk briskly. The hard run had pulled him into a comfortable euphoria, the runner's high nicely replacing the anxiety and turmoil that had been consuming his heart and head since discovering Joanne wasn't the woman he thought she was.

But then the questions returned. Who was Joanne Lake? Who had he fallen in love with? Who was that woman who'd made him feel like they'd been the king and queen sitting at the top of their own little world? Who was that divine creature who'd convinced him that no matter what the obstacles they could accomplish anything with each other? That without each other all was lost to them. Because he felt lost without her, and he wasn't liking the feeling one bit.

He'd asked those questions in prayer that morning, down on his knees at the altar. His aunt Juanita had pointed him back in the direction of Greater Bethlehem Baptist Church, the house of worship he and his brothers had attended since they'd been little boys. "Pray," she'd admonished, believing that prayer would give him the answers he was seeking.

He'd have preferred to keep his problem secreted away, but church had a way of exposing whether a person was doing well or not. Dressed in his Sunday best, prayer had provoked his tears to sneak past his lashes and down his face, and anyone who'd been watching had been able to tell that Luke Stallion wasn't doing well.

He missed her, and he couldn't deny it if he wanted to. He missed her laughter and the way she teased him when it was just the two of them alone. He missed their late-night conversations as they lay side by side in his bed cuddled close together. He would have given anything to hold her hand, her fingers entwined between his own. He loved her, and in that moment, all he could think of was how much he wanted Joanne to love him back.

"I think we should intervene," Marah was saying to John, the two curled together on the rear patio of their home.

"No," John responded emphatically, tightening his arms around his wife's torso. He hugged her warmly. "No, Marah. They have to work through this on their own."

"If our families hadn't intervened when they did, we might not be together right now."

John laughed. "We'd be together. It would just have taken your stubborn self longer to realize how much you loved me."

"Me? I knew I loved you. I was the one who flew all the way to New York to find you, remember?"

John nuzzled his wife's neck. "Yes, you did, and had I been in New York we would have made up sooner."

"That's why we need to intervene. You weren't in New York, and if our family hadn't helped we'd still be flying across the country trying to find each other."

"Perhaps, but we still are not going to interfere with Luke and Joanne, and that's final. The two of them will figure this out on their own."

Marah said nothing, a wicked smile pulling at her mouth. "Okay, honey. Whatever you say."

"I mean it, Marah Stallion. Leave Luke and Joanne alone."

"I said okay, John!" She tilted her face to his and kissed him quickly. "Whatever you say, baby!"

John laughed again, the hearty chortle echoing through the late-night air. "I swear, Marah," he said after catching his breath, "if you and your sisters even think about getting involved…"

Marah giggled, turning to kiss him again. Her smile was wide and full. She responded brightly. "Yes, dear, I understand perfectly."

Joanne refused to answer her father's telephone calls. Recognizing the number on the caller ID, she let out a frustrated sigh. The telephone rang six times before her answering machine finally picked up the call. After the message had played, Charles Lake's booming voice flooded the room for attention.

"Joanne, there's a package being delivered today. Sign the papers inside and then get them back to me please. This is important.

"And call me back, Joanne. I don't know what is wrong with you, but this is not the time for one of your tantrums. Call me, Joanne, and I mean it."

The phone clicked and a dial tone filled the room before the machine cut off. Joanne rolled her eyes, annoyance flooding her spirit. She fingered the large envelope sitting on her kitchen table. The deliveryman had knocked on her door just minutes before her father's call had come. Tearing open the envelope's sealed flap, she pulled a stack of legal documents from the inside. A yellow sticky note was affixed to the front, her father's scrawly handwriting reiterating his instructions. "Joanne, sign and return. Dad"

Flipping through the documents, Joanne's expression was suddenly contemplative. After reading through the contents, she jumped from her chair to reach for the silverware drawer. Grabbing the stack of envelopes inside, she tossed them onto the kitchen table and began to open each and every one.

What Joanne discovered was more than she had bargained for, and the knowledge was powerful. She couldn't begin to imagine what her father had been thinking.

As if reading her mood, the weather outside suddenly turned. Wind swept leaves and debris in a whirlwind. It grew noticeably in force, gusting hard against her windows. When the rain started to fall, pouring out of the sky, Joanne's tears fell with it, and then, just like that, both stopped, tears and rain finishing together.

Moving toward the back of the home, Joanne knew that somehow she needed to talk to Luke. She knew beyond any doubt that it wasn't going to be easy to accomplish, but she knew where to go to try. There were only a few people who Luke respected enough to listen to. She would start there, she thought, as she formulated a plan.

An hour later, dressed to impress, Joanne pushed the stack of paperwork into her leather briefcase. Grabbing her keys and cell phone, she rushed out the door, determined to fix what she'd managed to break.

Chapter 20

The Stallion airplane sat fueled and ready on the airstrip. When Luke's limousine pulled up, he was ready to take flight and Luke paused in the cockpit door to greet the pilot.

"We'll be ready to depart in a few minutes, Mr. Stallion," the man said.

"Thank you."

Passing his suit jacket to the stewardess and loosening his tie, Luke made himself comfortable in a leather seat. He pulled a folder of paperwork from his leather satchel, readying himself to get some work accomplished on the flight.

He still didn't understand why John had insisted he fly to their Atlanta offices to personally pick up documents that could just have easily been shipped via air express. But John had insisted, commanding Luke to honor the request.

Minutes later he gestured for the stewardess. "Is there a problem, Louise?" he queried, looking down to his watch. "We should have taken off by now."

"There's no problem, Mr. Stallion. We're waiting for one more passenger."

"One more? Who?"

"I'm not sure, sir. Your brother called and instructed us to wait for a second passenger. They should be here very shortly."

Luke nodded his head, reaching for his cell phone. He assumed one of his brothers had decided to join him. Dialing the office, he wanted to check which one was causing the delay.

Before the call was connected, Luke heard the stewardess greeting someone at the door. Turning about in his seat he was surprised to see Joanne coming into the cabin. He was even more surprised when she revised the flight itinerary, instructing the pilot with a new schedule.

"I don't think so!" Luke exclaimed, jumping from his seat. "What are you doing here?"

Joanne nodded her head toward the pilot. Behind them the copilot was closing the cabin door.

"Pilot, this woman isn't flying with us today."

"Yes, I am," Joanne stated firmly. "You really should sit down. We'll be taking off soon," she said as she eased past him, moving to the leather seat opposite the one he'd occupied.

Luke spun in the direction of the cockpit instead. "Pilot, shut this plane down now and escort this woman off the plane, please!" he exclaimed loudly.

The gray-haired man in the pristine uniform smiled politely. "I'm sorry, sir, but that's not possible."

"Excuse me?"

"We have explicit instructions from John Stallion, sir. I'm told the lady will explain." The man gestured with his head to the back of the plane. "You'll need to take your seat, Mr. Stallion. We've been cleared for departure."

Luke shook his head as he moved back to his seat. The entire time Joanne's gaze was locked on him. Avoiding her stare, Luke dropped down into his seat. He scanned the tabletop for the cell phone he'd dropped there. He lifted his folder, peering beneath it.

Reaching out her hand, Joanne pressed a warm palm against the back of his hand. She whispered his name. "Luke."

Snatching his hand back as if he'd been burned, Luke glared at her. "Where's my cell phone?"

Joanne smiled sweetly. "You're not going to need it."

"Excuse me?"

"Where we're going, you're not going to need it."

Luke sat back, his arms folded harshly across his chest. He took a deep breath and held it, trying to contain the rise of emotion threatening to explode from him. "What's this all about, Joanne? Why are you here?"

"We need to talk, Luke. This was the only way I could think to get you alone where you have to talk to me."

"Have to? Woman, I don't have to do anything. And the last thing I'm remotely interested in doing is talking to you."

Joanne locked her gaze on him. Exasperation fueled her words. "You really are a stubborn ass, Luke Stallion."

Luke bristled. He pointed his index finger at her, ire painted across his face like bad makeup. "When we get to wherever we're going, you had better find your own way back to Dallas. I'm sure your father will be able to arrange something for you. Until then, don't say one word to me. Not one word. Understand me?"

Joanne shook her head. "Don't you even want to know where we're going?"

The Gulfstream jet was sailing along at an altitude of 26,000 feet. They'd not been in the air for very long, and Joanne had already grown weary of Luke and his silent treatment. They only had another hour or so before they'd be landing, and he still refused to speak to her.

Luke had reclined his seat, lying on his side to face the window away from her. He'd dozed off to sleep or had pretended to. But what he wasn't doing was trying to make things better between them. Joanne shook her head. If nothing else, he was determined. His brothers had said he would be.

Joanne's morning conversation with John and Matthew Stallion had lasted almost three hours. It had taken her the first hour to tell them about herself and her father and to make them understand that nothing that had happened between her and Luke had anything to do with the takeover attempt.

She'd spent the second hour convincing them that she loved Luke more than anything else. She'd fought back tears trying not to let her emotions overtake the moment. There had been too much at stake. She'd been desperate for them to know that she had not lied. Everything important to her had depended on them believing that she had not betrayed Luke or the Stallion family.

The last hour had been spent planning. It had been her idea to steal Luke away for a little tête-à-tête. John had helped facilitate the finer details. Both brothers had hugged her warmly and wished her well. Now here she was trying to wear down the wall Luke had put between them.

Moving to the seat beside him, Joanne cradled her body around his frame. She wrapped her arms around his waist and gently caressed his arm, his side, his hip. She half expected him to pull away from her, and when he didn't, she pressed herself in closer, brushing her breasts and pelvis against his backside.

Luke kept his eyes closed tight. The woman's presence had knocked him off balance. Realizing his brother had helped her pull off this little transgression surprised him completely. And he was still angry, still confused, still searching for answers. But for the moment he was relishing the sensation of her hands, having missed her touch like he'd not missed anything before. So he didn't open his eyes. He didn't move at all, allowing himself to linger in the moment of her sweet caress and hold on to it for all it was worth.

"So, are you ready to talk yet?" Joanne asked softly, still drawing a path against his shirtsleeve.

Luke took a deep breath. He shifted his body against the seat, moving to lift himself up and turn himself around to face her. His anger had cooled substantially. Now he was simply curious, more questions spinning through his head than should have been allowed.

"Why did you lie to me?" he asked, finally meeting her stare. There was an edge to his voice, the wealth of it rapping at Joanne's confidence.

"I didn't lie…or at least, I didn't mean to. I'm more guilty of omitting the truth. I never said much about myself or my family at all. You formed your own conclusions based on what folks from the center were telling you."

"So, where did you grow up?"

"In Kessler Park."

"With your parents?"

"Just my father. My biological mother lives in Paris. I spent one month out of the year there with her."

"So you speak French?"

Joanne giggled as she nodded her head. *"Oui, je parle français."*

"Who is Mrs. Brooks? And Marley?"

"She was our housekeeper but had more to do with raising me than anyone else. Marley is her daughter and my very best friend."

"So why the deception?"

Joanne spent the next half hour trying to explain to Luke what growing up with Charles Lake had been like. She spared him no details about her life, even chastising him for assuming things about her based on what folks at the center had told him.

"They really don't have a clue," Joanne said with a quick shrug. "I didn't want my wealth to be an issue for me with the clients."

Luke nodded his head slowly. "So just how wealthy are you?"

A slow smile pulled at Joanne's mouth. "When and if we ever need a prenuptial agreement, I'll let you know."

Luke laughed. "The girl's got jokes!"

"I have a question for you," Joanne said softly.

Luke eyed her curiously. "So ask it."

"Why did you turn your back on me? Why wouldn't you talk to me? We both said how important it is for us to communicate with each other. Why would you do that to us?"

Luke paused. "Because I was afraid that me letting my guard down had jeopardized what my brothers have built over the years. You have to understand, Joanne, they raised me. I'd have nothing if it wasn't for Mark, Matthew and John. Especially John.

"And I let my guard down with you. I trusted you because I believed in us. I was afraid that I had made a horrible mistake and they were being made to pay the price, as well. It would have been one thing if you'd used me and I lost something. It's something all together different if my whole family has to suffer."

Joanne shifted her body from his, replaying everything he'd just said in her mind. Tears swelled full and hot against her eyelids. She brushed the saline away with the back of her hand. Luke drew a finger along her face, pausing to cup a palm beneath her chin. He lifted her face until her stare met his intense gaze.

Joanne fell deep into the loving look. The dark reservoirs were hypnotizing. A faint bead of perspiration beaded on Joanne's top lip. Leaning toward her, Luke motioned as if he intended to place a kiss upon her lips, but he didn't. Joanne gasped softly, her own mouth quivering with anticipation. But his lips never met hers, the pilot coming over the intercom to interrupt them.

"Ms. Lake, we've been cleared for landing, ma'am. If you and Mr. Stallion would please fasten your seatbelts. Thank you."

Joanne pulled back slightly, her gazed still locked with Luke's. The stewardess came to check on them both before returning to her own seat. Luke leaned his shoulder against Joanne's. He moved his mouth next to her ear and whispered.

"So, just where have you kidnapped me to?"

Joanne allowed a wide grin to bloom across her face. "Kiawah Island."

Chapter 21

Joanne had been enamored with Kiawah Island since she'd been a little girl. She'd been nine years old the first time she'd visited the South Carolina low country, one of few vacations she and her father had actually shared together. With its ten miles of pristine beach, sun-washed rivers and marsh and abundant wildlife and nature, it had become one of the best places for her to spend her time.

Joanne had loved Kiawah so much that on her eighteenth birthday her father had gifted her the multimillion-dollar property on Flyway Drive. The home was oversized, sitting on nearly two acres that boasted 180 feet of bulkhead along the expansive waterfront. The main house had an adjoining two-bedroom pool house and a 225-square-foot lighthouse-inspired watchtower. It was more house than Joanne would ever need for herself alone, but it was a welcome place to lay her head at night when she visited.

Joanne could tell by the expression on Luke's face as he

took in the expanse of landscape around them that Kiawah had grabbed his attention just like it had grabbed her.

Stepping from the rental car, Joanne watched him as he gazed out over the water, inhaling the scent of salty oceanic air. The midday temperature was exceptionally warm, a brilliant sun sitting high and full against an equally exquisite canvas of bright blue sky.

Luke abandoned his necktie and jacket completely as he made himself comfortable. He undid the top buttons of his white dress shirt and rolled up his long sleeves. "This is nice," he said, following behind her as she headed for the front door of the home. "Very nice."

Joanne tossed him a quick glance over her shoulder. "Thank you. This is one of my favorite places in the world to come to."

Luke nodded his understanding as he stepped through the home's entrance behind her. Looking around, he took in the home's heart pine floors that extended from the foyer into the great room with its mahogany ceiling and beams, stone-surround fireplace and three sets of French doors that opened onto an expansive patio and deck.

Luke stepped out onto the deck, which overlooked the marsh. Joanne followed behind him.

"This place is haunted," she said with a soft chuckle. "Kiawah was originally inhabited by the Kiawah Indians. They say the British came in and purchased it for a sum of cloth and beads. When the British took over, the land became inhabited by hundreds of African slaves on two plantations. Hundreds of black men, women and children died here, and it's whispered that their spirits roam through the lagoons."

Luke's eyebrows were raised as he listened intently. When Joanne had finished, he shook his head. "I swear, woman, you'll say anything to get me into your bed," he teased, a sly smirk on his face.

Joanne laughed. "I'm not afraid of ghosts. You're the one who likes to sleep with all the lights on."

He laughed with her. "And if you ever tell anyone, I'll deny it completely."

She shook her head. "My lips are sealed."

Changing the subject, Joanne moved toward the rear door. "We need to run into town to get some food. There's nothing in the pantry and even less in the fridge."

Nodding, Luke followed her back inside and out the front door.

Luke pushed the grocery cart as the two meandered through the grocery store. As Joanne collected the staples that would last them for their extended weekend, Luke tossed sugary junk food into the cart that they really wouldn't need.

"I swear!" Joanne exclaimed, removing a box of chocolate crunch cereal from the carriage. "You don't really eat this stuff, do you?"

"This stuff is good. It flavors the milk chocolate," he said, putting the box of cereal back in.

"But I'm cooking French toast for breakfast."

"This isn't for breakfast. This is for a snack."

Joanne smiled, shaking her head. "You're killing me!"

An hour later, after the food was situated in the large kitchen pantry and the refrigerator, Luke was pouring himself a large bowl of chocolate-flavored flakes. He poured a second bowl, covering it with milk and pushing it across the counter toward Joanne.

"Taste this. This is the best."

Still shaking her head, Joanne lifted a spoonful to her

mouth, slowly savoring the flavor. A wide smile pulled at her lips. "This is so wrong," she said, laughing. She took a second mouthful, settling herself on the cushioned stool beside him.

Luke's mouth was full, milk dripping over his lips, as he nodded his agreement. "But so good," he said after swallowing.

Two bowls later, they both pushed their dishes away from their bellies and themselves away from the counter.

"That was dinner," Joanne said.

Luke rolled his eyes. "That was an appetizer. Food foreplay for us connoisseurs of fine dining."

Joanne crossed her arms over her chest. "Really? Food foreplay?"

The man grinned, his expression teasing. He leaned in toward her, his voice dropping to a deep whisper. "You do remember the foreplay, don't you, Joanne?"

Joanne felt her breath slipping from her. Heat suddenly flooded her body, belying the cool air filtering from the central air conditioning. The silence grew thick and heated between them, until Luke chuckled heartily, breaking the quiet.

"Why don't you show me where I'll be sleeping," he said, rising to his feet. "Before it gets dark and I see a ghost or something, okay?"

Joanne laughed with him. "I definitely wouldn't want you to get spooked."

Luke grabbed her hand, clasping her palm beneath his own. "Me neither."

As she gave him a tour of the house, heated anticipation seemed to tease her senses. Joanne found herself quivering with anxiety. Despite their rising comfort levels, the man hadn't made any overtures for something more romantic.

As he stood next to her admiring the second-floor master suite with its his-and-her walk-in closets, lush spa bath with gold limestone countertops and the beautiful gas fireplace, she'd wanted nothing more than to strip them both naked and make love right where they stood.

Instead, she watched as Luke surveyed the surroundings before asking if there was a second bedroom on the floor.

She nodded. "Yes, it has two master suites."

Guiding him to the end of the hallway, she opened the door to the second bedroom. Luke walked the room's perimeter, admiring the apothecary-influenced cabinetry, granite shower and impressive marsh views.

Turning to face her, he was suddenly overwhelmed. Her expression mirrored the wealth of emotion he was feeling. He'd hated the tension that had split them one from the other. He'd missed her so hard that it had felt as if he'd lost his heart, the muscle ripped from his chest. Now he was hungry for her. He'd been fighting the sensation since she'd stepped on the plane, and now, as she stood staring at him, his restraint was failing him. He took a step in her direction and stopped.

The longing that had risen between them was tangible. It was overwhelming and copious, leaving both of them shaking with anxiety. Luke took a second step when Joanne turned abruptly, almost racing back to the other end of the hall.

"Joanne!" Calling her name softly, Luke moved quickly behind her, catching her by the arm. He gently pulled her back to him, wrapping his arm around her waist and holding her close against him. "Joanne!" he whispered into her hair, brushing his lips to her forehead.

Joanne closed her eyes, allowing her body to relax into his. Tears suddenly burned hot against her lids. Luke's strong hands closed around her waist as she spun around in his arms. Pressing her back against the wall, Luke dropped his mouth to hers, his kiss urgent with desire. Joanne's hunger kissed him back as she wrapped her hands around his neck. Eager tongues danced one against the other as roving hands glided from one body to the other.

Luke's attention moved to her shoulder, pushing her blouse out of his way as he trailed wet kisses to mark his path. He reversed his course, meeting her mouth a second time. Neither was interested in relinquishing their embrace of the other, both holding on for dear life. Then Luke paused, taking a step away from her. His eyes had misted as he stared deep into her gaze.

"I'm sorry," he whispered, contrition seeping from his stare. "I should have trusted you, and I'm sorry I didn't. I don't want anything to ever come between us again. I love you so much!"

Joanne's tears slipped past her lashes, dampening her cheeks. Luke wiped the moisture from her face, his fingers gently caressing her cheek. He kissed her again and then pulled her along beside him as he moved into the bedroom.

Laying her gently against the mattress, Luke stood tall, staring down at her. She was angelic, sheer perfection personified. Joanne's mouth was parted slightly, desire seeping from her gaze. It was obvious that she wanted him as much as he wanted her, and his appreciation pressed hard and firm in his slacks.

Sitting upright on the edge of the bed Joanne parted her legs wide enough for Luke to stand between them. She clutched the back of his thighs, her fingers grazing his buttocks as she pressed her face to his abdomen. She kissed his belly button, her heated breath burning hot against his flesh.

Luke clasped her face between his hands, dropping his mouth back to hers. His kisses were soft and sweet, intermingled with gentle, light caresses that crossed her shoulders and billowed down her back. Words weren't needed to express the emotion sweeping between them, her moans and his sighs speaking volumes for them both.

Luke pushed her back against the bed. He eased his knee against her side, lifting himself above her heated body. Kissing her through her clothes, he pulled at the buttons that held her blouse closed, then undid the straps of her brassiere until all her secret charms hidden beneath were fully exposed. Dropping his body down against hers, he resumed his kisses against her bare flesh.

Starting at her belly, he kissed his way up to the luscious mounds above, running his tongue from one to the other. The wetness of his kisses as he lashed at the nipples, which had bloomed full and hard, sent tiny ripples of delight through Joanne's body, cascading over her spirit.

She whispered his name again and again, the sweet mantra like music to his ears. Pulling at her clothes, Luke stripped her naked in no time. Equally eager, Joanne tugged at his shirt and the waistband of Luke's slacks until she'd freed him from the confines of his clothes. His naked beauty was intoxicating and Joanne inhaled him, drinking in every square inch of his incredible physique.

Dropping down onto the bed beside her, they lay side by side, their bodies interlocked as they kissed and caressed each other, savoring the sensations being drawn from their bodies. Luke explored hidden recesses and Joanne stroked hardened flesh. Both were damp with perspiration, succulence attesting to their excitement. The moment was simply surreal.

A mutual exclamation filled the warm evening air. Outside, the sounds of mating echoed their lovemaking, seeping through the opened window. Joanne would have sworn the wildlife was singing them a love song.

Luke sheathed himself, the quick gesture coming before she'd even realized he had pulled away from her body and was back again. She cried at the pleasure of his entry, arching her back off the bedside as his sex kissed her own.

Bodies pressed tightly together, they rocked back and forth against the massive bed. Sweat dripped into sweat as short, breathless pants spilled from their mouths. The resounding waves of passion grew quickly as one body fed from the other, both nourishing the other's rising need.

The sweet music of his moans and her cries filled the night air. Again and again, Luke pressed himself into her, his strokes deeper and deeper, filling her with ripples of lust that exploded in quick, heated bursts. When neither one could take another minute of the pleasure, Joanne screamed his name and Luke screamed hers, both writhing in ecstasy.

From where she stood on the deck outside, she could hear him sleeping soundly, his breathing heavy. He inhaled deeply, then exhaled, his snores low and deep as his chest heaved up and down. Moving back inside the bedroom, Joanne stood in the doorway watching him.

The blankets had tangled around Luke's feet, the taupe-colored bottoms shining in the dim light. He looked peaceful and relaxed, his expression content. The warmth of their bed beckoned her back beneath the covers, but she needed a few more minutes of quiet before she went.

The alarm clock on the nightstand blazed its neon lights into the darkness. It was shortly after three o'clock in the morning and Joanne hadn't been able to sleep as soundly as Luke seemed to. She'd risen from the warmth of his body and had wrapped herself in her silk bathrobe. Slipping her pedicured feet into a pair of oversized slippers, she'd been drawn to the outside and the cool, early morning air.

Moving back outside, Joanne stared out over the landscape. A quarter moon barely illuminated the outdoors. Night sounds swept through the darkness. Joanne wrapped her arms around her torso, hugging herself snuggly.

Closing her eyes, Joanne said a prayer of thanksgiving. She had much to be grateful for. She and Luke were slowly rebuilding the connection between them. But she understood it wouldn't happen overnight and it wouldn't happen quickly. Communication was coming slow and steady as the two rediscovered the balance that had existed between them.

Making love to the man had been a sweet release. His touch had moved her spirit and invigorated her desire to make things well between them. Luke had touched her heart like no man before him. She loved him and she would do anything to show him how much of her heart belonged completely and totally to him.

Back inside the bedroom, Joanne eased herself back into the bed, drawing a sheet up and over both their bodies. She turned to face him, curling her body close to his. Adjusting the bedclothes over his shoulders, Joanne tilted her head up to kiss that spot beneath his chin.

She was surprised when Luke reached out and wrapped his arms around her, drawing her closer to him. A sleepy smile curled at the edge of his full lips.

"Everything okay?" he whispered softly.

Joanne nodded her head into his chest. "Everything is perfect," she said warmly.

Giving her a quick squeeze, Luke brushed her hair against his cheek. "I love you, Joanne. I never stopped. And even when you thought I didn't, I did."

* * *

For three straight days, Joanne and Luke wrapped themselves around each other, quenching a thirst for something neither had realized they needed. The atmosphere was soothing, detoxing the frustration and anger that had existed between them.

Luke stared out over the upper deck of the home, watching as Joanne slowly strolled the outskirts of the property. He smiled as she stopped to stare up at him, waving her hand in greeting. Above them both, a large bird cawed in a tall tree, the creature voicing its annoyance at their intrusion.

Young love had gripped them hard, both so enthralled with each other and the thought of where their love might take them that they could think of nothing else. Thoughts of family and friends intruded ever so briefly, the fleeting emotions quickly dismissed with a kiss, a caress or a look. Luke savored the feelings.

Watching her in that environment, Luke felt a sense of home like he'd never known before. It was comfortable and engaging, moving him to want to do and be better for her. They'd spent hours nestled together, talking about their future, their individual dreams entwining together into a singular, common goal. He now understood fully what Mark and John had wanted him to understand about the intricacies of love.

As he'd been lost in thought, Joanne had made her way back inside the home. She joined him on the porch, two bowls of chocolate cereal in hand.

"I thought you might like a snack," she said as she passed him a dish.

Luke smiled. "You're hooked now, aren't you?"

Joanne laughed. "I am not hooked. We just need to finish

off the milk before we leave," she said as she spooned a mouthful past her lips.

"Admit it. You're hooked. I told you this stuff was addictive."

"Okay," Joanne said as she ate another mouthful. "It might be kind of addictive, but once we're finished with this box we're quitting cold turkey. My hips can't take but so much of this junk."

Luke laughed warmly. "I'm sure your hips will be just fine."

The plane ride home was as quiet as the plane ride there. This time though, the wall between them had imploded, nothing left of it but the last molecules of dust billowing through the air. As they sat in silence, they touched with their eyes. With a simple gaze, Luke had caressed the length of her arms, her shoulders, the nape of her neck and the small of her back. Sheer pleasure had risen deep within her as she felt him enveloping her in his arms. The two sat intoxicated by the swell of emotions sweeping between them.

Sometime later, as the plane continued to soar through a mist of bright white clouds, Joanne reached for the briefcase she'd left in the aircraft's overhead compartment. Pulling the large envelope from inside, she laid it on the tabletop and pushed it toward Luke. He looked from her to it and back again.

"What's this?"

"You're going to need these for the meeting tomorrow."

"I don't understand."

"My father likes to buy me things. Things that will be good for my future. This envelope contains statements detailing the shares of Stallion stock that my father purchased for my future. You're going to need these for the vote. I was supposed to sign over power of attorney to my dad so that he could vote them on E-Kal's behalf, but I never did.

"Also inside is my signed proxy giving that power of attorney over to you. You might need it to win this battle. Do whatever you have to do with them to help you and your brothers."

"Joanne," Luke exclaimed excitedly, his hand falling atop the folder. "Are you sure about this?"

Joanne smiled, leaning over the table to press a kiss to his lips. "I love you, and I am more sure about that than anything else in this world."

Chapter 22

A special meeting of the Stallion shareholders had been called to vote on the E-Kal bid to take control of Stallion Enterprises. The hotel conference room was filled to capacity. Edward, Juanita, Marah, Mitch and Vanessa sat in the rear of the room, listening intently. Joanne sat in the front row, one leg crossed over the other, her gaze cast down to the floor. Every so often she'd stare up at Luke and smile.

Luke and his brothers sat side by side as they listened to Charles Lake plead his case before the hundred or so interested investors. John had already gone over the state of their business operations, boasting of their substantial profit margins and increased productivity within all the company's divisions. He'd also stressed his capability and ardent willingness to continue running the company to the best of his ability. But concern still blanketed the older three brothers, who sat tight-lipped and tense. Luke, however, was the epitome of calm, cool and collected.

Mark leaned to whisper in his sibling's ear. "Hey, you spent the weekend with the woman. You couldn't get her to change their minds?"

Luke smiled, shrugging his shoulders.

John hushed them both. "Shhh."

Mark shrugged, his expression questioning. "Aren't you even a little worried?" he whispered to Luke.

Luke shook his head. "No. We got this. Didn't John tell you?"

"Didn't John tell him what?" John asked, leaning into the middle of their conversation.

"About the stock."

"What stock?"

Energy flushed Luke's face. "Didn't Joanne speak with you last week?"

John nodded, his voice barely audible. "We talked about you, yes. What else was there for us to talk about?"

Luke smiled. The man at the podium tossed a glance in their direction as he continued to rant. Luke's smile widened as he gave Joanne's father a slight nod of his head. This time he shushed his brothers.

"Be quiet. That's my future father-in-law speaking," he said, crossing his arms over his broad chest.

Mark rolled his eyes as John heaved a deep sigh. Matthew cut his eyes from one to the other, his head shaking slightly from side to side.

From where she sat, Joanne watched them all. Her gaze lingered on her father, whose intensity was engraved in the lines that creased his forehead. The two had encountered each other in the hallway, the man barely bothering to say hello before questioning why she was there.

"Why am I here?"

"You really don't need to be here, Joanne. All you needed to do was sign the papers I told you to sign."

Joanne had nodded her head. "I thought I should be here, Daddy. I mean, like you said, this is *our* company. And since I own fifty percent of *our* company, I think it's past time I became more involved. Don't you agree?"

Dr. Lake had shrugged. "More involved, huh? Whatever, Joanne. I really don't have time to argue this with you right now. Did you bring all your bonds and your voting documents?"

"Yes, sir, I did."

"Well, when it's time, I'll tell you what to do. Okay?" Without waiting for her to respond, he'd kissed her forehead, rushing to extend his hand in greeting to another of the Stallion shareholders.

Joanne shook her head. Still standing at the podium, her father was concluding his argument, seemingly confident that he'd won all the stockholders and their votes over. His gaze met hers ever so briefly, and Joanne smiled. Charles Lake didn't bother to smile back.

Calling for a brief recess before the official vote, the meeting's moderator asked for a motion and a second, both of which were received. The noise level in the room suddenly increased tenfold, chatter rising quickly. Moving off the stage, Luke made his way to Joanne's side, wrapping his arm around her waist. She met his stare.

"Joanne, I love you. I love you very much, and it's very important to me that you don't do anything you really don't want to do just to please me. I love you for wanting to give me your shares and your vote. But I don't want you to go against your father just because you're angry at him."

"But I'm not—"

Luke held up his hand, stalling her comment. "Yes, you are. You're angry because you love him and you've spent most of your life questioning his love for you. That's the wrong reason for you to be doing this.

"You own valuable shares of Stallion Enterprises. If you vote for the regime to stay as it is, then you need to do it because you honestly believe that's the right thing for the company and for your interests in the company and not because you and I are in a relationship.

"Baby, I love you and no matter what happens, you and I will survive this. So—" Luke paused, passing that large envelope back to her "—these belong to you. Vote them as you see fit."

Kissing her cheek, Luke winked at her as he made his way back to the stage. Taking a deep breath and then another, Luke moved to Dr. Lake's side. He extended his hand in the man's direction.

"Dr. Lake, if I may have a moment, please."

"Mr. Stallion," the older man said, moving to shake Luke's hand.

"Please, call me Luke."

"What's this about, son?"

"Dr. Lake, I don't know if you're aware or not, but I've been dating your daughter. I just wanted you to know that I love her very much. And I support her in everything she wants to do. Joanne's happiness is the most important thing to me, and right now, she's not very happy at all.

"Sir, Joanne loves you very much, but you really need to work on your relationship with her. I know you love her, but Joanne doesn't seem to trust that, and she should.

"My father died when I was eight years old. I really don't remember him. Every day I think about what I missed not having him around. My older brothers are all I had. You are all Joanne has, and I don't want you to lose her."

The patriarch bristled slightly. "Who do you think you are talking to me like this?"

Luke smiled brightly. "Dr. Lake, I'm your daughter's future. And that's going to make us family. If I didn't learn anything else from my brothers, I learned that family always comes first."

With a quick nod of his head, Luke excused himself, making his way back to his brothers.

John eyed him curiously. "What was that all about?"

Luke smiled. "Just chatting with my future father-in-law."

Nodding his head with understanding, John smiled back.

Her father was sitting in her living room waiting for her when she returned home. As Joanne stepped over the threshold, the two locked gazes. The man's expression was blank, not an ounce of emotion shining from his eyes.

Joanne hung her purse and suit jacket over a closet doorknob. Moving into the room, she took the seat opposite him. The two continued staring at each other, neither saying a word.

Tears suddenly brimmed at the corners of Dr. Lake's eyes. He took a deep breath, swallowing the emotion before blowing a gust of hot air over his lips. "Have I really been a horrible father to you, Joanne?" he asked, his voice cracking ever so slightly.

Joanne shrugged her shoulders. "You've always been too busy to be horrible, Daddy. You've always been too busy to be a father at all."

Her father nodded his head slowly. "Estelle Brooks called me. She blasted me good," he said with a soft chuckle. "She doesn't think I was much of a father, either." He ran his hand across his head. "So, tell me about this young man of yours. Mr. Stallion seems very sure of himself."

"Luke is an amazing man, Daddy."

Her father nodded again. "It would seem that he loves you very much."

Joanne smiled, falling into a moment of reflection. Her father watched her, his expression thoughtful.

Shifting forward in his seat, his elbows resting on his thighs as he clasped his hands together in front of him, he said, "I was very proud of you today, Joanne. That little speech you gave was quite impressive."

Joanne met her father's gaze.

He continued, "Everything I have ever done, Joanne, I have done for you. But clearly I've made some serious mistakes." He sighed deeply. "I hope," he said, reaching for his daughter's hands and clasping them between his own. "I hope you'll give me a chance to make up for that. I hope you'll let me show you how much I truly love you."

Joanne eyed him with some skepticism.

Her father voiced her concern. "I know you might not believe me," he said softly. "I'm sure you're asking yourself why."

Joanne nodded. "Yes, I am actually. Why now, Daddy? What's changed?"

Her father wrapped his arms around her shoulders and hugged her tightly. "A wise man told me that family has to come first."

The Stallion family was gathered together at Briscoe Ranch celebrating their victory. Smiles were wide and bright, accolades and congratulations ringing through the evening air.

Sneaking over to her husband's side, Marah looped her arm through his. John pressed his mouth to hers, greeting her with a warm embrace. She shook her head, shaking an index finger in his direction.

John laughed. "What? What did I do?"

"I thought you said we weren't supposed to intervene," she said, cutting her eyes up at him.

John smiled. "No, I said *you* weren't supposed to intervene."

Marah laughed. "So why did you get to have all the fun?"

John feigned ignorance. "I don't know what you're talking about, Marah Jean."

"Oh, yes you do. From what I hear, Luke didn't manage to get on board that Stallion jet with Joanne without someone's intervention."

The man shrugged. "Really? I wouldn't know anything about that."

"Sure you don't."

"Really," John said, his expression less than convincing.

Marah smiled. "Well I'm glad you didn't intervene, and I think your brother is, as well."

They both stared across the room in Luke's direction.

"He looks happy," John said softly, squeezing his wife against him.

Marah nodded her agreement. "He does. As a matter of fact, all you Stallion boys look happy," she said thoughtfully.

Across the way, Luke tapped Matthew on the shoulder. "Hey, bro, can I borrow your car? I need to pick up Joanne."

Matthew shook his head. "Where's yours?"

"Stuck between Marah's Mercedes and that tank Mark is now driving," Luke said, referring to his brother's new SUV.

Matthew reached into his pocket for his car keys. He passed them into Luke's hand. "Don't crash it. It's only a loaner," the man said, smiling.

Luke nodded. "So, what's the deal with yours? Can they fix it?"

Matthew grinned. "That baby is beyond repair. The insurance company totaled it. I need to buy me a new one. I just haven't had time."

"What happened to the kid who was driving?"

"The courts will hear his case in the next few weeks. He was only fifteen years old."

Both men shook their heads.

Matthew changed the subject. "That was a ballsy thing your girl did today. We were impressed."

Luke paused, reflecting on the meeting and the vote. No one expected Joanne to ask for the floor, demanding an opportunity to speak to the room. The moderator had insisted a motion be made to allow them to stray from protocol. Luke had made that motion, all his brothers seconding the request. Joanne's father had escorted her to the stage, a wide grin filling his face. Then Joanne had spoken and that grin had faded quickly. The memory of Joanne's comments spun through Luke's head.

"The CEO of E-Kal Development Corporation and the CEO of Stallion Enterprises have both made viable cases for control of Stallion Enterprises corporate helm. Clearly, the Stallion family brings a formidable track record to the negotiating table. Their strength and determination are what have made their company the lucrative enterprise that it is.

"I have a vested interest in both businesses, and I want to see my stock investments do well. My decision and vote are based on what I believe is best for E-Kal and Stallion. Both have been led by amazing management teams, but one brings something to the table that the other doesn't begin to possess.

"Stallion Enterprises needs to be run by a management

team with heart. A management team that continues to believe in its employees and who will fight tooth and nail for the good of the company first and foremost. In all my research I wasn't able to find one business decision made by the Stallion family that wasn't based on ensuring the sovereignty and well-being of their core values. Every decision has been made on mutual respect for their staff and their investors. Every acquisition was based on their overwhelming love for and belief in this company.

"Regrettably, many of E-Kal's corporate decisions have been based on values less honorable and with little consideration for what was best for their shareholders.

"In consideration of this, I vote my interest in Stallion Enterprises to John Stallion and his family. I hope that you will all follow suit. I hope that your decisions will be swayed by what is best for our investments and not tactics of coercion and dissuasion. Thank you."

Joanne had moved to her father's side after that, gently kissing his cheek before returning to her seat. After that, the vote had been unanimous, every stockholder pledging allegiance to and belief in the Stallions.

Luke grinned. "My baby is something special."

Matthew clapped him on the back. "And she has herself a very special guy. Don't ever forget that. Now go get your girl and bring my car back here without a nick or scratch on it."

Chapter 23

Luke entered the luxury jetliner shaking his head. "You have a jet, too?" he said, tossing Joanne an amused glance.

"This one's my personal plane," Joanne answered, laughing softly. "I also have a boat. A very big boat."

Luke grinned. "Sweet. My prenup is looking better and better," he joked.

Joanne laughed. She settled down in the seat beside him. Luke wrapped both his arms around her and hugged her tightly. He held her close as the plane moved from the tarmac to the runway.

"So, where are we disappearing to this time?" Luke asked, looking out the window as the plane lifted high in the air.

Joanne smiled. "Paris. I want you to meet my mother."

Luke's head bobbed up and down against his thick neck. He leaned to kiss her mouth, his lips gliding gently across her own. "Hey, Joanne," he whispered against her mouth, the warmth of his breath teasing her senses. "I need to ask you something."

"You can ask me anything," Joanne whispered back as she brushed the warmth of her cheek to his.

"What are you doing for the rest of your life?"

Joanne smiled. "Did you have something special in mind?"

"Mmm-hmm," Luke murmured. "I'm hoping you'll want to spend the rest of your life with me."

She smiled, a full grin spreading across her face. "I think that might be arranged."

Luke nodded, kissing her a second time. "Good, because I like how you do things, Ms. Lake."

Joanne chuckled. "I'm glad to hear it, but I think I'm getting the better end of that prenuptial, Mr. Stallion."

"Really? How do you figure?"

"Lost in a Stallion's arms forever! What else could a girl ask for?"

Luke hugged her close. "I love you," he said softly.

Joanne nodded, snuggling closer to him. "I love you, too!"

The moment between them grew quiet as they drifted into a state of contentment with each other. The plane soared higher and higher against a backdrop of deep blue sky and a spattering of whitewashed clouds. Luke nuzzled his face into her hair, kissing the top of her head.

He thought back to the beginning, the day he'd met Joanne for the first time, sensing that something was going to change his life forever. He'd been right, and he'd been wrong. He was a true Stallion, through and through, but love had clearly bested them all.

REQUEST YOUR FREE BOOKS!

2 FREE NOVELS
PLUS 2 FREE GIFTS!

KIMANI
ROMANCE™

Love's ultimate destination!

YES! Please send me 2 FREE Kimani™ Romance novels and my 2 FREE gifts (gifts are worth about $10). After receiving them, if I don't wish to receive any more books, I can return the shipping statement marked "cancel." If I don't cancel, I will receive 4 brand-new novels every month and be billed just $4.69 per book in the U.S. or $5.24 per book in Canada. That's a saving of over 20% off the cover price. It's quite a bargain! Shipping and handling is just 50¢ per book in the U.S. and 75¢ per book in Canada.* I understand that accepting the 2 free books and gifts places me under no obligation to buy anything. I can always return a shipment and cancel at any time. Even if I never buy another book from Kimani Press, the two free books and gifts are mine to keep forever.

168 XDN E4CA   368 XDN E4CM

Name _____ (PLEASE PRINT) _____

Address _____ Apt. # _____

City _____ State/Prov. _____ Zip/Postal Code _____

Signature (if under 18, a parent or guardian must sign)

Mail to **The Reader Service:**

IN U.S.A.: P.O. Box 1867, Buffalo, NY 14240-1867
IN CANADA: P.O. Box 609, Fort Erie, Ontario L2A 5X3

Not valid for current subscribers to Kimani Romance books.

Want to try two free books from another line?
Call 1-800-873-8635 or visit www.morefreebooks.com.

* Terms and prices subject to change without notice. Prices do not include applicable taxes. N.Y. residents add applicable sales tax. Canadian residents will be charged applicable provincial taxes and GST. Offer not valid in Quebec. This offer is limited to one order per household. All orders subject to approval. Credit or debit balances in a customer's account(s) may be offset by any other outstanding balance owed by or to the customer. Please allow 4 to 6 weeks for delivery. Offer available while quantities last.

Your Privacy: Kimani Press is committed to protecting your privacy. Our Privacy Policy is available online at www.eHarlequin.com or upon request from the Reader Service. From time to time we make our lists of customers available to reputable third parties who may have a product or service of interest to you. If you would prefer we not share your name and address, please check here. ☐

Help us get it right—We strive for accurate, respectful and relevant communications. To clarify or modify your communication preferences, visit us at www.ReaderService.com/consumerchoice.

KROM10